Book One in The JACK REACHER Cases

CLICK HERE TO BUY NOW

MOLLY

A WADE CARVER THRILLER

DAN AMES

Published by Slogan Books, Inc., New York, NY.

FREE BOOKS AND MORE

Would you like a FREE copy
of my story BULLET RIVER?

Then sign up for the DAN AMES BOOK CLUB:

For special offers and new releases, sign up here

MOLLY

A Wade Carver Thriller #1

by

Dan Ames

"Killing the time between corpses..."

O FLORIDA, VENEREAL SOIL

-Wallace Stevens

D elray Beach sounds like a nice place.
Anything with the word 'beach' in
it usually does. Unless it was Hell
Beach. Or Herpes Beach.

Delray Beach, though? Pretty good.

Del, meaning 'of' in Spanish. 'Rey' translates to
King.

The King's Beach.

Not quite.

Oh, the beach is nice and there are a few funky
little historic houses here and there but some of
the city-planning chowderheads decided not to
bother enforcing regulations for drug and alcohol
treatment centers. Meaning, any Tom, Dick and
Cocaine Harry could set up shop calling them-

selves a treatment center. Have some beds, throw a few brochures at the junkies you encourage to crash at your place, and you can bill the insurance companies five grand a week, *per person.*

Recently they busted one of these guys who was raking in over a hundred grand a month by scamming the insurance companies on his 'treatment centers.' Here's a clue. The guy was driving a Lamborghini. Even better? He was a full-force drug user and alcoholic. The cops busted him doing over a hundred miles an hour on the freeway. Once the newspapers got hold of the story, his days running a treatment center were over.

Anyway, thanks to the city's lax regulations, the situation has gotten pretty bad. In fact, there are places in Delray Beach where the treatment houses fight over the derelicts. They troll the bus stations for derelicts with at least one form of genuine identification.

How do I know all this?

Well, I live here now, part-time. I've got a place up in Michigan on a little island in a corner of Lake Huron. It's my favorite place in the world up there, although winters do get a bit long and in the summer you've got to deal with the deer flies.

Those bastards will bite you through your shirt and draw blood.

My jobs have brought me down to Florida a few times and feeling those warm ocean breezes in the middle of February, accompanied by some rum, beer, or both, is quite pleasant.

So I bought a home here in Delray Beach.

And set up an office not too far away.

Not just because it's The King's Beach.

No, I'm here for a more practical reason.

It's the last place my sister was seen alive.

2

"Mr. Carver?"

She was a damn good-looking woman. Older than me by at least five, maybe ten years. She was blonde, but with highlights that probably cost what I spent per week on groceries.

Her eyes were blue, lips wearing just a hint of pink and perfect white teeth. Her face was classic, an elegant jaw line, fine nose and the bearing of sophistication.

She wore a sundress, with sandals and her toenails were painted a light pink.

She was tall, and that caught my interest immediately. Tall women have a way of spotting weak men who are easily intimidated.

I'm not weak.

And of the emotions I might feel being in the presence of a tall, good-looking woman, intimidation ain't one of 'em, if you know what I mean.

In my experience, a tall woman appreciates that.

"Depends who's asking," I said.

"My name is Margaret," she said. She cocked her head slightly to the side, and took in my office.

My place was a building from 1967, the Summer of Love. It was white, with circular exterior patios that reflected a contemporary modern aesthetic. At least, that's what the real estate agent told me.

Whatever.

I bought the tenth floor penthouse because it had a front room I could use as an office, and in the back it had a double patio that provided views of both the open ocean, downtown Delray and the intercoastal.

Many days I would lock up the front office, and sit out on the back patio with some drinks and good music. Not a bad way to spend winter. Much better than hunkering down against wind chills twenty below zero, taking the occasional break to shovel snow.

"What brings you here, Margaret?" I asked.

The choice between answering my question and leaving was in her eyes. Hiring a private investigator was an iffy proposition for a lot of people. Something shady about it, furtive.

A small percentage of prospective clients would back out of the office at this point. Claim they had the wrong address. Those were cases of a much more personal nature. A cheating spouse, usually.

It was the ol' chicken out and bail. Not that I could blame them, it was probably similar to going to a therapist for the first time. Telling a complete stranger your worst secrets.

No fun at all.

I watched Margaret weigh her options.

I gave it a 50-50 chance. A soft exhalation of breath and I caught the scent of coffee and citrus.

Margaret pulled out a chair across from my desk and sat down.

"I've heard your specialty is finding and retrieving women."

"Put it that way, I sound like a dog breed."

"Specifically," she said, ignoring me, "young women who may have some issues with drugs."

Margaret didn't have a wedding ring. No tan

line from one either, which was not the case more often than you might think.

"I don't know if you'd call it a specialty," I said. "But I do have some experience in that regard."

"Good, because I need help. From someone like you."

When she said that, her eyes gave me the once-over.

I know what I look like.

Not the prettiest creature God put on this green earth. A misspent youth left me with some scars and some facial features that weren't exactly classic. But I was packed with muscle, especially broad in the chest and shoulders, and occasionally people crossed the street when they saw me coming.

Men and women alike.

"I'm not a cheap date," I said. The fact was, I had money in the bank from some of my past activities, and when I didn't have a paying gig, I continued to search for my sister. I had spent years and a small fortune trying to find her, but I would never give up.

Sometimes, though, it required multitasking.

"Good, I don't like cheap men," Margaret said. She withdrew a folder from her purse, which was an orange thing made of leather. I could tell it was an expensive deal, but it was well-worn. A woman who pays for quality and doesn't discard it.

She placed the folder on my desk.

"I did some research and you come recommended," Margaret said. "I'd like to hire you for a week to start. If it takes longer, we can talk about it."

"What do you want me to do?"

"Find my daughter."

Margaret closed her eyes and the next few words rang with the echo of rapidly disintegrating hope.

"Her name is Molly."

3

The tall woman's full name was Margaret Hornor, at least, that's what it said on the check she gave me. It was a nice chunk of change and represented a retainer for me for a week. She also signed a new client form that doubled as a contract.

"I'm going to need a few more things, as well," I said.

"You name it," Margaret answered.

"For starters, usernames and passwords for all of her social media accounts and email, if possible. Her cell phone number and even better would be her usage bills. If you give me the login for her wireless account, I can analyze her calls and texts as well as the numbers they were sent to."

Margaret had taken out a neat little leather portfolio – who knew they made pink leather – and jotted down my requests.

"I'll also need a list of friends, boyfriends, anyone in her inner circle. Full names and phone numbers if you have them."

It was interesting the way Margaret wrote. Smooth, unhurried, with bold, confident strokes. Her perfume had managed to fill my office space and it was like a warm ocean breeze tinged with eucalyptus had somehow wafted its way inside.

My guess is Margaret had been an athlete. A little too tall for soccer, not beefy enough for softball. That left basketball or volleyball. Maybe a swimmer.

"Other than you, does she have family in the area?" It was an honest question, with the added benefit of asking about Molly's father. The man who was most likely Margaret's ex, by my educated guess.

"No," Margaret said. "Her father lives in California. Her sister is going to college in Massachusetts."

"Harvard?" I asked.

Again, another guess. There were a lot of colleges in Massachusetts. When a parent is telling someone they just met about a college-aged student, they almost always say the name of the school. When Margaret failed to mention it, I figured it was either a really expensive school, or a desire for privacy. My guess had been the former.

"Yes," Margaret said. "How did you know?"

"Process of elimination."

She didn't know quite what I meant but I didn't expand on my answer.

"Has she ever gone missing before?" I asked. "Extended periods of time away from home without telling anyone where she was? A lack of communication for more than a few days."

"Of course," Margaret said. "She's got a problem. She would go out and often not come home at all. But when she did finally drag herself back, it was almost always within twenty-four hours. I think there was only one time it was longer than a day, and that was a weekend where she went out on Friday and didn't come home until Sunday."

"How long has it been now?"

The first change in my client's demeanor appeared. Just a subtle shift of facial muscles changing the expression from professional determination to sorrow.

"Three weeks."

"Have you been to the police?"

"Yes."

"So they're looking for her, too?"

"They claim they are, but Molly had been arrested a couple of times. Once for drunk and disorderly. Another time for minor possession. I think once they saw her record, they assumed she was out partying. This is south Florida, after all."

"You don't think she's out partying, though?"

"Anything is possible," she said, without resignation. "Either way, I want you to find her and bring her back."

Margaret stood, and she was only a couple inches shorter than my 6'3". She held out her hand, I took it. A strong grip. Cool.

Definitely an athlete.

"Please keep me updated as much as you can," she said, and then she hesitated.

"Full disclosure?" she asked.

"That's the best way."

"I hired you because of your reputation. I'm afraid my daughter may have fallen in with some people who are a level above your average substance abusers."

She sounded so clinical. Probably the way she

was forcing her way to think about it to keep her emotions in check.

"I won't do anything illegal," I said. Of course, that was complete and total bullshit. Someone famous once said that the more laws we have, the less justice. Cicero, I think.

"And I wouldn't ask you to," she said.

There was a slight smile on her face.

It matched the one on mine.

Two people lying to each other, knowing what each is doing.

It was sort of romantic.

4

There are no basements in Florida.

This is something I learned recently. So where does everyone put their crap, the kind of detritus most people in the Midwest put in their basement?

The garage.

They fill their garages, often times to the brim. It's not uncommon to drive around a Florida neighborhood and see people with their garage doors open, revealing mountains of boxes, furniture, shelving units and sporting goods.

You know what you never see in Florida garages?

Cars.

So to fit in with the locals, I decided to put my home gym in the garage.

In my line of work, it's fairly essential to be in good shape. I'm not the fastest guy in the world, but I can run at a steady clip for miles and miles, and if I catch you, not even the good Lord can save you.

I've got mostly free weights and a heavy bag that I beat the hell out of every other night.

After the visit from my tall-drink-of-water new client Margaret, I closed up the office, went home and put in a good workout. Now, dripping with sweat, I chugged from a huge, ice-cold bottled water.

The place I'd chosen for my Florida home was a ranch house from the 1950s. It was all open, with an all-white kitchen, basic, comfortable furniture, and a great room that opened out onto a pool.

The pool was going to be my next stop, but my cell phone buzzed and I fished it out, checked the screen.

Hammerhead.

A bizarre little guy with a smashed-in face that I often used for information on the street scene, up and down the east coast of Florida. He had a lot of connections, everywhere except in his brain. He'd fried so many synapses that people often wondered if he had Tourette's syndrome.

"Wade!" Hammerhead screamed at me.

Wade isn't my real name. But sometimes I need a name to put on official paperwork, and here in Florida, that's the name I came up with, when I was standing in two feet of water just walking around.

"Jesus, stop screaming," I said.

"I'm in deep shit!"

"I'm not a plumber."

"No, no. Not literally. I mean, I'm in trouble."

With my free hand, I slid open the glass sliding door, stepped out onto the pool deck.

"Good," I said.

"Good? No, it's not good! It's bad!"

I slid off one shoe and sock, dipped a toe in the water.

Perfect temperature.

"Being in trouble is good," I said. "Sharpens your senses. Makes you feel alive. Hey, I have another call coming in."

Not true. I hung up on Hammerhead, went inside to my bedroom and looked for my swimming trunks.

Hammerhead called back.

"Wade, you've got to come over here. They think I stole from them and they're going to do God knows what to me."

"Did you?"

"Did I what?"

"Steal from them."

"No! These guys are nuts! They want me to sell for them and they're pretending I ripped them off, but it's bullcrap. You need to help me."

He lowered his voice.

"My Mom is here. They said they would...do things to her."

That made me stop. For starters, I knew Hammerhead was very close with his Mom. She kept bailing him out, and he depended on her.

Two, nothing pisses me off more than street thugs hassling a woman. And it really gets under my skin if it's an older woman. All the shit she probably dealt with her whole life, and what's the reward? To get hassled by some drugged out scumbags?

No, I didn't think so.

"Ok. On my way."

No need to shower. I threw on a black T-shirt, jeans, and a pair of black trail shoes.

I left the shirt untucked, so I could slip my

every day carry, a .45 semiautomatic pistol with an 8-round magazine, into a concealed holster in the back of my jeans.

Along with the gun, I slid a spring-loaded knife made by some recluse in Idaho. The knife wasn't cheap, but the blade can cut through bone.

Out in the driveway, I climbed into my car, a 1976 Ford Maverick. It was black, with oversized rear tires and had been totally rebuilt from the ground up, according to my specifications. The guy who had done the work was a genius whose life had exploded when his wife died and his daughter disappeared. I helped him put his life back together, starting by finding his daughter and bringing her back.

He paid me with the Maverick.

The engine was insanely powerful and the wheels were equipped with huge brakes to keep things under control.

Now, I cruised over to Hammerhead's place, a tiny house on a street littered with garbage, rusty vehicles and fallen palm leaves.

I pulled slightly onto the shoulder of the road, and parked the Maverick partially on the neighbor's yard directly across from Hammerhead's house.

There wasn't room to do it on my informant's side, because it was already filled with cars.

One of them was a huge black truck with over-sized wheels and a "Florida Cracker" decal in the corner of the back window.

It looked like Hammerhead's colleagues had beaten me to the punch.

So to speak.

5

There was a little sign in the flower bed next to the front door. It said: 'Make yourself at home.' There were no flowers, of course, just weeds and cigarette butts.

Nevertheless, I took the sign's advice, opened the front door and stepped inside.

"Whoa!" said a big, sweaty white guy in a wife-beater shirt and barbed wire tattoos that wrapped around his oversized arms. His head snapped around to look at me.

His partner, a little weasel of a guy in dirty jeans, a stained Corona beer T-shirt and cowboy boots, started to walk toward me.

And then he stopped.

I figured the big guy was the owner of the truck, the one with the Florida Cracker sticker. He had a big meaty paw on the forearm of Hammerhead's Mom.

It looked like he was trying to snap it in two.

Hammerhead had seen better days. His nose was bleeding, he had a cut on his forehead, and half of his face was swollen. He was sprawled out on the ground, his back against a curio cabinet filled with Precious Moments figurines.

"Get the fuck back out through that door," the Cracker said. "If you know what's good for you."

"Didn't you see the sign out front?" I said. "Make yourself at home. That's what you're doing, right?"

"Squirrel, get rid of this guy," Cracker said.

The smaller guy looked at me, and clearly wasn't crazy about the order from his boss.

"Have to get better at identifying species," I said to the big guy. "I thought your little friend here was a weasel."

It's tough being commanded to take the lead on a project with a fairly high possibility of failure. I could see it in Squirrel's eyes. He was probably pretty wiry, maybe even quick, too.

But animal cunning isn't limited to Wild Kingdom. There was a sense in his feral little eyes that he was facing a legitimate threat, one that he had to weigh against the known dangers of disobeying his superior.

It was plain to see his thoughts: Is this guy scarier than Cracker?

The trouble was, I was an unknown quantity. Whereas, Squirrel probably had a very good idea of Cracker's capabilities.

So he came at me, slid a big old Bowie knife from his waistband.

Nice knife, I had to admit. The steel looked good. Military-grade black handle. Seemed to have a very fine edge on it.

It would be a nice addition to my collection.

To stab a man, even for a psychopath, usually requires motivation. More than just being told to get rid of someone. When you stab someone, there's a pretty good chance they'll die, unless you purposely slash an arm or a leg, avoiding main arteries.

Still, it wasn't something to take lightly.

There was hope in Squirrel's face. Hope I would see the knife and duck back out the door.

But like my gal pal Emily Dickinson wrote, 'Hope is the thing with feathers.'

I threw a straight right that caught Squirrel flush on his jaw. It was unexpected, and even though he was quick, he was too surprised to duck.

Plus, he had a knife. Which, in terms of blocking a punch, confuses the issue. He kept his knife where it was and tried to block it with his other hand. But my fist drove right through and pole-axed him.

He sagged and I twisted the knife from his hand and kicked him in the balls. He sank to his knees while I reloaded my fist and I whipped a right hook that nearly tore his jaw from his face. I heard a nice cracking sound and suddenly Squirrel had a whole new look. *Unhinged* would be the proper adjective.

Cracker dropped the old lady's arm like it was on fire.

He held both of his big meaty hands up in the air.

"Whoa," he said.

"Impressive vocabulary."

"We're just getting some money that's owed to us."

I stabbed him through his palm. Again, I had a

nice element of surprise. The Bowie knife was enormous. The blade was ridiculously long and it had been little more than a flick of my wrist.

Remember that part about how a man needs motivation to stab someone? Well, I wasn't being totally truthful.

I don't need a lot of motivation.

A big jackass beating up an old lady is good enough for me.

He howled and grabbed his hand.

"Take your Squirrel and go," I said. "Come back and I'll slit your throat."

Up close, Cracker was a weird-looking dude. A smashed-in kind of face that he tried to cover with a big beard.

"Don't make another mistake," I said as I watched him try to get his hand behind his back to where I knew there was either a gun or a knife. Maybe both.

He stepped past me and I snatched the big revolver that was stuffed down the back of his jeans.

A ridiculously heavy Colt .44 Magnum.

"Unoriginal, too," I said.

Cracker dragged his pet Squirrel out of the house and I followed them to the door. They barreled away in the big black truck and I locked the door, turned to Hammerhead and his Mom.

The old woman looked down at her son, then up at her curio cabinet.

"Son, don't you dare break my Precious Moments."

6

"Get it together, man," I said to Hammerhead. "Jeez. Have you no shame? That white side of beef was going to break your Mom's arm."

He was now on his feet, and his Mom had gone into her bedroom to lie down. Being roughed up by drug dealers tended to fatigue the elderly, according to AARP.

Hammerhead wiped the blood from his face with a kitchen towel.

"Don't put it back in the sink," I said to him as he was in the process of doing just that. "And while you're at it, clean this place up."

It looked like he was going to cry.

Hammerhead was really not the right nickname for him. He was a little guy, who at some point in his life may have been muscular but now he was kind of thin and his muscles were atrophied. He was probably in his thirties but looked like he was old enough to qualify for Medicare.

"Don't cry. There's no crying in drug dealing," I said.

"Jesus, man," he whined. His voice was like a broken flute in desperate need of a spit valve repair. "Cut me a break! I mean, thanks for getting rid of those guys, but I'm not in a good place right now."

What a damn whiner.

"Not in a good place?" I asked. "You're in your Mom's house for Christ's sake. It's not the place, it's *you*. No matter where *you* are, you're screwed. Know what I mean?"

He went to the fridge and grabbed a beer.

"Why don't you go see if your Mom needs something?" I asked. "Always thinking of yourself first, Hammerhead. That's the sign of an addict. Selfish."

He went down the hallway and I heard her yell at him. He came into the kitchen like a beaten dog.

"She doesn't want anything right now," he said.

"Of course not, why did you go bother her?"

I admit, I was having fun tormenting him.

"Very big of you to thank me for saving your life" I said. "You owe me one. And I'm going to collect right now."

His shoulders sagged. Like it was too much trouble for him.

"Would you rather I call those guys back? Let 'em finish the job?" I said.

"No, no. That's fine. What do you want?"

"Molly Hornor. A girl. She's missing. May be hooked on something."

"You think I know every junkie chick in Delray?" he asked, spreading his little hands wide. "There's frickin' hundreds of 'em. New ones show up every day."

He had pulled a beer from the fridge, twisted off the cap and drank half of it in three big gulps.

"You always ask your guest if they'd like something to drink before you start swilling beer?" I asked. "God, you've got horrible manners and your selfishness is reaching new heights."

"You want a beer?"

"Of course not," I said, still messing with him. "Listen you little ingrate, here's what you're going to do."

I went and got the ridiculous Colt revolver,

dumped out the bullets and pocketed them, and handed the knife to Hammerhead.

"You're going to take these spoils of war to a pawn shop. You're going to get some cash, and use it to buy information. If there's a little left over, you can buy your mother some flowers. Of course, I know you won't. You'll probably buy yourself some drugs because you're a sad excuse for a son. But let me tell you something. You'd better buy that crap only *after* you've gotten the information. Or I will be very upset."

Hammerhead's mood had suddenly improved.

His eyes lit up at the prospect of getting his hands on some cash.

I picked up the knife and put the tip against his Adam's apple.

"You're going to call me before you get stoned, with my information. If you don't have it, I'm going to do your Mom a favor and cut you into little pieces and put them on display in the curio cabinet, next to her other Precious Moments."

From the back bedroom I heard a noise.

She was clapping.

7

I n my line of work, a little extra security was fairly important. So once I'd pulled the Maverick into the garage, I went inside, locked up, and set the alarm. No ordinary security system. Multiple cameras, safeguards, even a few extras.

My urge to go for a swim had passed so I settled for a scalding hot shower to wash away any traces of Florida Cracker and Squirrel, along with the dried sweat from my workout. I had a walk-in shower in my master bedroom, with a steam deal that was mixed with menthol. It cleared the head.

After throwing on a pair of cotton shorts and a T-shirt, I detoured to the kitchen for a glass filled with Tito's Vodka and a splash of sparkling water with a lime. My nightly vitamin.

My house has an open concept – the kitchen has a long island with counter-high leather chairs. Beyond the island is a rustic farm table with six chairs. To divide the room, a white couch sits with its back to the farm table, flanked on either side by vintage side chairs, facing a fireplace with a mantle on which sat a flat screen television.

The sliding glass doors that opened out onto the pool were closed, with the shades drawn. They were also coated with reflective film to prevent any aggressive voyeurs, or former antagonists who were having a problem letting go of the past.

Ice clinked in my glass as I sipped the vodka. The flat texture of the vodka was enlivened by the carbonation of the water, and the hint of citrus reminded me just how much I enjoyed being in Florida.

Lately, I'd been fooling around on Tinder, just for fun. It's a phone application where single people can find other singles. It's super simple: photos appear and if you swipe left on the photo, it means you're not interested. If you swipe right, it means you like what you see. If that person then swipes right on you, you both get a message saying 'It's a Match!'

From there, you can set up a date.

I'd met a few women via Tinder, and had some fun. Then again, most of my history with women was a cavalcade of sinful pleasure, short on meaning and resonance, merely brief rest stops on the journey forward.

There was an abundance of divorced women in Florida, and I seemed to do well with them. Maybe they were looking for someone like me after a decade of misery.

Now, I used the app and started swiping. Their faces peered up at me from my phone. A lot of plastic surgery. One caught my eye. A brunette. I loved brunettes.

Swipe right.

It was interesting to see the poses, the expressions, how a person chooses to present themselves to the world. It was a few minutes of diversion and as my vodka was nearly gone, I told myself to swipe one more.

The face looked back at me and I smiled.

Margaret Hornor.

She had the same no-bullshit look she'd worn in my office. I read her bio. She made a point of mentioning she was tall and a former athlete. Short, fat guys need not apply, although she didn't come out and say it.

My thumb hovered on the phone screen.

Swipe right meant I was interested.

If I swiped left, she would be gone from my options.

It would be fairly unprofessional to swipe right. Then again, she might never see my profile.

Maybe it was the vodka, or maybe I had intuited something more than I was admitting.

I swiped right.

There was the briefest of moments as my screen dipped into black.

And then a message appeared.

'It's a Match!'

8

Everyone's got "their" spot at the beach. Myself included. It's a little picnic table just up from the hip and trendy downtown area of Delray Beach, but just before you get to the ultra swanky section of private homes that represent a chunk of wealth equal to Ecuador's gross domestic product.

This morning, the picnic table was empty. There were a couple reasons for this. One, it was fairly early. Two, it's become a bit of a habit for me to stop by there and have some good strong morning coffee. And three, my presence seems to frighten away a certain segment of the population.

So I once again took my spot at the table, a good cup of coffee in hand, and watched the waves roll in. I sat sideways at the table, though, so I could keep one eye on the road and sidewalk behind me.

The breeze was fantastic coming off the water, a bit of grit and salt mixed together. It was too early for the sun to be a factor and it was a perfect temperature, not too hot, not too cool. A few seagulls fought over a Kit Kat wrapper nearby.

Every time I came to the ocean I thought about my sister. It was what had drawn her to Florida in the first place.

That, and our broken home.

Jenny was older than me by two years and it was a fact that had caused a lot of pain. I always felt that on some level she felt she had to be my protector, but that was impossible in the situation of our youth. Our Dad was a cop, who was killed on the job, and our Mom was a neurotic, driven further into mental illness by the loss of her husband.

It was chaos.

My Mom was gone, and I was determined to find the subhumans who had murdered my father in the line of duty. I dropped out of school, already a brawler, and learned everything there to know about fighting with fists, guns and knives from my Dad's cop friends, who were also hunting his killers, after-hours.

Eventually, I found the men responsible, and exacted justice, gleefully dumping their bodies into the Detroit River, like expelled feces from a ruptured sewer line.

By then, I was a terror, and Jenny was gone.

Lost in a swirling mixture of alcohol, drugs, and a manic desire to escape. She was fleeing Detroit, the memories of her parents. And, frankly, me.

It wasn't until later I realized how much her feelings of shame and failure at not being able to protect me, drove her to make the choices she did.

That was the real tragedy to me. There'd been no reason for her to blame herself. It was no one's fault.

It was life.

The sound of shoes scuffling on the sidewalk interrupted my train of thought and I saw Hammerhead strolling up toward me. He was clearly stoned, as Jim Morrison would say, 'immaculate.'

"Perfect day to catch some waves, man," he said to me. My guess was that Hammerhead hadn't surfed in years. The drugs were giving him the impression that he was someone he wasn't. Isn't that why so many people got hooked?

"Perfect day for some information," I said. "What do you have?"

He stretched out on the picnic table and stared up into the early morning sky.

"The Candyman can 'cuz he mixes it with love and makes the world taste good," Hammerhead sang.

"You're about to start tasting your teeth, piece by little piece," I said.

Hammerhead swung his feet down and looked at me. "That's his name. The Candyman! Dude wears bright orange shorts like the waitresses at Hooters! Blonde-haired guy, with a girlfriend from up north who goes by Molly Chambers."

"That's a song by Kings of Leon," I said. "Molly's Chambers."

"What can I tell you? Bro's the biggest dealer around Delray Beach, I guess. You said you were lookin' for a girl named Molly and that she's a junkie. I made the *connection*," Hammerhead said, and pantomimed the bringing together of two things and then he made an exploding sound and his fingers danced through the air.

"Where does the Candyman sell his goods?" I

asked and drained the last of my coffee. There was a recycling bin next to the picnic bench and I threw my cup inside.

"No idea, but I heard he goes to Narcotics Anonymous meetings to lure people back onto drugs. There's a daily meeting around noon that he never misses, what I heard."

"Why don't you make your Mom happy and go to one of those meetings?" I said. "Might do you some good."

He started singing again and I left, walked back to the Maverick, and fired it up. I scrolled through my phone until I found the song Molly's Chambers. I played it through the car's sound system, the irresistible beat pounding like a freight train as I cruised down the A1A, the ocean off to my left.

"Molly's Chambers gonna blow your mind..."

9

The cop stopped me.

Actually, *the sight* of the cop stopped me.

No, I wasn't speeding. And no, the cop didn't pounce on my tail and try to goad me into speeding so he could give me a ticket.

This was an entirely different kind of traffic stop.

A filthy camper had been pulled over on Swinton, just west of downtown Delray Beach. It was in the part of town that started to get closer to the freeway, which meant the neighborhood got worse.

In some cases, a lot worse.

The cop was standing, hand on hip, talking to two weird-looking guys, both wearing camouflage and sporting long beards.

There was a parking spot available and I slid the Maverick into it, and then watched.

Officer Paula Barbieri was a looker, even in dark blue polyester pants and shirt. She had dark hair she usually kept short, but now it pulled back in a pony tail and looked a little longer than normal. Her parents were Colombian and she had darker skin, with fiery black eyes.

Ordinarily, you might think a guy like me would go out and see if the officer needed assistance.

Nuh-uh.

If anyone needed help, it would be the two clowns in the dirty camper if they tried to mess with Officer Barbieri.

And mess they did.

The guy on her left came in at her to get in her face and she did a beautiful leg sweep, brought him down on his face where it met the concrete sidewalk. It sounded like someone threw a Christmas ham off a high roof.

The second guy stood frozen, which was the right move.

Barbieri cuffed the first guy and then told the second guy to get on the ground, which he did.

Her next move would be to call for back-up, which I saw her do, leaning her head down to speak into her radio. And then she would clear the camper.

That would be the tricky part.

Now, I was tempted to help, but I stayed put.

Which was a good thing. Because when Officer Barbieri went in the camper, a gnarly-looking black guy with a gun came out the back. For a moment, I thought he was going to circle around and try to shoot her, which would have meant that it was time for me to get involved.

Instead, he jumped out and ran right toward me.

Now, I'm no hero. Never have been, never will be. But something about the sight of a man running down the street with a gun, about to go right past me, just didn't sit well.

The Maverick is an old car. Built with heavy steel, back when no one even pretended to care about fuel economy. Plus, it's a two-door. So the one big driver's door actually weighs quite a bit and packs a fairly good blow when it's flung open as hard as possible, as I did just then.

The door slammed into the man's solar plexus and dropped him in his tracks. I had followed the door on its way open and stepped on the man's wrist, grinding my foot into his bone. The gun clattered to the asphalt and I kicked it away with my foot.

That's how Officer Paula Barbieri found us.

She walked up to me and stopped.

Rolled her eyes.

"Wade Carver, fastest car door in the West," she said.

A glance at my door showed me there wasn't even a mark from the fleeing suspect. But I pretended there was.

"Will your department cover that?" I asked.

"Are you nuts?" she replied. "We have to buy our own Kevlar vests, for Christ's sake. I can't expense a taco."

Another squad car arrived and Barbieri cuffed the guy on the ground.

"A threesome," I pointed out.

"You wish," she answered.

"Drinks tonight? That coconut martini you like at Sidu?"

She thought about it.

"Lemme see how the paperwork goes," she finally said.

It would have been nice to hear a little more enthusiasm.

10

As far as I could tell from my online research, there was only one Narcotics Anonymous meeting in Delray Beach, and it was held in a giant room at the rear of a strip mall, with nothing on the door to indicate it was a meeting place for substance abusers.

Nearby there was a hair styling boutique, a pizza place and a shoe store. That made sense to me. Once you got free of drugs you'd probably want a fresh haircut, some pizza, and a new pair of shoes.

Once, a few years back, I went with a former client of mine to an Alcoholics Anonymous meeting, to help her put her life back together again. It had reminded me a lot of church. It opened with some readings, then there was a lecture in the middle, and then another reading at the end.

Inside, the place was about what I expected. Mostly cheap plastic chairs scattered around, a few tables, and some inspirational quotes on the wall. There was an old-school coffee urn at the back of the room, along with a sink and a jar of sugar.

I sat down at the back of the room and waited.

It was an interesting parade of humanity that soon began to pass before me. All ages, all genders, all ethnicities. Some looked like they had just finished up a bender, others like they'd been clean for years and now successful.

What I really wanted to see was a guy in tiny, tight orange shorts. Like a male Hooters waitress.

No such man appeared.

By the time most of the seats were filled, a wiry little black woman brought the meeting to order and read some announcements, before people took turns reading from a book. And then the main speaker told his story about hitting bottom, and eventually finding a way out. They read some more, and then the meeting finished with people passing a donation basket. I added a few bucks.

Mostly, I kept watching the door, hoping to see the Candyman.

But he never showed.

A few of the people stayed behind while the others shuffled out, firing up cigarettes before they were even out the door.

Eventually, the wiry black lady was alone at the front and I approached her.

"Good meeting," I said.

She looked up at me. "They're all good as long as people show up. I haven't seen you here before, have I?"

"Nope, first time," I said.

"Well, I'm glad you came," she said.

"What's your name?" I asked her.

"Donna."

"I'm Wade."

We shook hands. "I tried this meeting out because a buddy of mine highly recommended it. They call him the Candyman, he wears orange shorts all the time. You've probably seen him around."

"You mean James?" she asked.

"Yep, that's him."

"No it's not," she snapped at me. "That was a test and you failed miserably. You're a cop. Trying to bullshit me because you assume I'm a drug addict and probably brain-addled. Get your punk ass away from me before I knock your teeth out."

She looked like she meant it.

I retreated and joined the others at a little outdoor area where most of them were chain-smoking.

"Man, you don't mess with Donna," a guy said to me.

He looked like Jimmy Buffet without any hit songs, restaurants, or money.

"Thanks, Captain Obvious."

"If you see Candy, tell him I need to talk to him," beat-up Jimmy Buffet said.

"He told me to meet him here," I said, going with the same lie even though it hadn't worked the last time. "But he was a no-show, obviously. I'm kinda pissed at him."

"My guess is he's down at the Oasis," my new friend offered.

"Is that a bar?"

"Nah, it's a housing complex that looks the other way, if you know what I mean. I think they call themselves a treatment facility, but it's not. It's a non-stop party is what it is, but you can get your shit messed up down there."

"And it's called the Oasis?"

"Yeah, funny isn't it?"

"Hilarious."

Downtrodden Jimmy Buffet peered up at me from bloodshot blue eyes. "You a cop? You sort of look like a cop."

"Nah. I'm a fashion designer. I pay Candy to wear my shorts I designed. Sort of like a celebrity endorsement."

Jimmy Buffet's less fortunate twin shook his head in disappointment.

"Not so sure that's very good advertising," he said.

11

Greek food never held much appeal for me until I discovered Zorba's. A place about a mile from my condo, with outdoor seating, a kitchen where people are always cursing at each other, and some damn fine food. Plus, you were allowed to bring in your own booze.

It was lunch, so I didn't show up with any hooch. Instead, I ordered a gyro salad from a waitress that continued to intrigue me. She was older than me, with honey-colored hair, a roundish pretty face and a great smile. She had perfect teeth and a fine body. Plus, she had that look. That one that says there's a lot more there than you might first suspect.

As I ate, my phone buzzed with incoming text messages.

From my client, Margaret Hornor.

She was looking for updates, and I figured she wasn't talking about our connection on Tinder.

I tapped out a message: *Following up on a few leads. Will call you tomorrow.*

After that text message was sent I went back to Tinder to look at Margaret's profile, but it looked like she had "Unmatched" us.

Suddenly, I felt the presence of someone hovering.

I looked up, and the waitress was looking at my phone. Probably at the Tinder logo.

"How is your salad?" she asked me.

"Delicious, thank you."

"How is your dating going?" she said, lifting her cute little chin at my phone.

"Not good, I keep looking for you but haven't come across your profile."

A smirk.

"I'm right here. Why are you looking there?" She had a little bit of an accent, and I could tell that English wasn't her first language. But she had learned it well.

"You're working, I didn't want to bother you," I offered. Pretty lame, really.

"Keep looking, maybe you'll find me," she said. "You need more water?"

She splashed some water into my glass before I could answer.

It seemed like a good time to put the phone away, so I slid it into my pocket, and proceeded to demolish my salad.

When I was done and she brought my check, I asked her name.

"Sofia. What's yours?"

"Wade."

She flashed me a dynamite smile.

"Please come back," she said. "I would love to have you."

Sofia left, making me wonder if a) her command of the language wasn't that great and her last statement was just awkward, b) she had full command of the language and meant exactly what she said or c) I really had to get out more.

My instinct's vote was clear.

C.

12

The Oasis was anything but.

No big shocker there.

From the dirty sign out front, to the two shabby guys sitting on the curb near the complex's front office, to the general sense of a Soviet-era work camp, the Oasis had seen better days.

If it had ever seen any good days at all.

The Maverick's powerful engine growled at the homeless-looking guys as we passed them and I parked in a spot that featured a curb with the word *visitor* barely visible.

I got out, locked up the car and heard the sound of The Offspring. Pretty Fly (For A White Guy).

Hmm. That song was a hit in the late nineties. It made me wonder if a junkie had gotten hooked on drugs back then and never moved on. Stunted both mentally, physically and perhaps worst of all, musically.

"Hey man, can you spare five bucks for the bus so I can get to my job?"

One of the homeless guys had worked up the guts to hit me up for money, but when I turned and he got a really good look at me, he kind of shuffled back to his spot on the curb.

There were eyes on me, all right.

A few windows here and there failed to fully camouflage the faces staring out. Lookouts? Worried about vice cops, probably. Maybe a few stoned, looking out at the day's sky like it was a tapestry of wonder and intrigue. Once the drugs wore off, the sun would be nothing more than the source of oppression and cruelty, sending them in search of chemical relief.

Inside, it smelled like piss and stale cigarette smoke.

There was a little office ahead and to the left. On the wall to my right was a bulletin board, mostly empty except for a calendar which was six months behind. On the wall to my left was a

Jefferson Airplane concert poster, torn through the center so the two halves hung crookedly.

The floor was dirty linoleum, and I followed a vague trail of foot traffic to the office where I found a woman probably in her seventies, with bright white hair piled on top of her head. She had a bright orange face, either burned from the beach, a tanning booth or spray-on tan. The effect was that she looked like a slice of carrot cake with a flower of frosting on top.

"I'll be honest, I'm not interested in renting one of these spectacular units," I said. "Although I do love the name. The Oasis. Reminds me of that Garth Brooks song."

"Fill out the form," she said to me, ignoring my opening gambit. "Don't lie, because we'll check."

"What do I get for filling out the form? Or is it a surprise?"

She looked up at me with tired eyes. Even her eyes look sunburned.

"You a comedian? There's been no one funny in this world since Lenny Bruce died," she said. "And you don't look like Lenny Bruce."

"No, I run all of the Florida Hooters restaurants and I'm looking for Charles, also known as the Candyman. We're going to hire him as the first male waitress. The publicity will be huge and he can make some easy cash. Maybe help him with his rent here, which I've heard he's very far behind on."

Naturally, I was improvising. Just throwing out some vague guesses but judging by the expression of the Carrot Cake Lady, I wasn't far off.

"Oh yeah, you mean the weirdo in 11. Yeah, he's almost always out by the pool is all I can tell you," she said, snapping her chewing gum. "Had to chase them out of there the other day. We get all kinds here but when the Haitians show up, you know they're up to no good. They'll steal your socks while you're wearing your shoes. Maybe even sacrifice a chicken or cut up a goat. They love goats, did you know that?"

It came out of her like a torrent.

"No, didn't know that about the goats."

"Yeah, well, some of 'em smell like goats, too. I really need to get a new job, I heard the Cracker Barrel up the street is hiring. The gift shop, you know, not the restaurant part."

"You'd be great there," I said, backing out of the office. "I'm heading over to the pool."

She pointed a big red finger to the right.

"It's over there," she said. "Just past the workout room no one uses."

"Ah, thank you."

Carrot Cake was right. The workout room looked like a storage closet where someone had put an exercise bike from 1970 and a lone pair of dumbbells. Five pounds each. The carpet looked filthy and someone had knocked over a bag of garbage.

I began to brace myself for what I might find at the pool.

Happily, I walked down the hallway and through a pair of double glass doors and I was outside. Fresh air. Tinged with chlorine.

There was a circular fence around the pool with a gate that had been knocked off its support posts and was jammed open.

To my left, I saw the Maverick surrounded by a few Oasis residents, checking it out. Through the gate, I arrived on the pool deck and saw a skinny black girl stretched out in a lounge chair, and next to her, a flabby white guy in bright orange shorts.

He was looking at me through a pair of Elvis-style sunglasses. Suddenly, he sat upright, jumped to his feet.

And ran.

13

For a brief moment, I watched with bemused detachment as the Candyman tried, and failed miserably, to execute an athletic endeavor.

He was pasty-white, flabby with no muscles whatsoever, wearing tight orange shorts and flip flops.

It was like watching a viral video, but it was live.

The Candyman flip-flopped his way to the fence, tripped over a pool chair and tried to vault the fence.

Only one leg managed to get over and he screamed as a stray flange ripped a jagged furrow into the bottom of fleshy white thigh. He kind of hung in the balance, part of his body in the dirt on the other side of the fence, one leg and a flip flop raised in the air.

His legs were spread wide providing a view no one, least of all me, wanted to see.

It was easy to cross the pool deck, use a small table as a stepping stool and hop over the fence. I looked down at the Candyman.

He wasn't crying, but he was close to it. His foot was stuck in the fence and his Elvis sunglasses were askew.

"Let me guess, you ran track in college as a high hurdler," I offered.

"What do you want? I don't have anything on me!" he said. His voice was high-pitched and panicked. He was older than I thought, seeing him up close. Probably in his forties. His skin was dry and lined and he had bad teeth. Yellow and crooked.

All the hallmarks of a meth user.

"No kidding you don't have anything on you. Put some clothes on for Christ's sake," I said. "Here's a free tip: the amount of exposed body should match the level of physical attractiveness. You're in severe violation, pal."

"What the hell are you talking about?"

"Molly Hornor," I said. "Where is she?"

"Who?"

"Molly Hornor. You're her dealer, right? Where can I find her?"

His leg finally popped loose and he rolled free and staggered to his feet. Threw his shoulders back, adjusted his sunglasses.

"I'm no one's dealer, you fricking caveman," he said. "Why don't you get out of my face?"

It seemed that regaining his composure had also sent a shot of adrenaline into him. It was kind of funny to see.

He raised a finger and started to point it at my chest.

"I don't think you're a cop so you can–"

Unhurried, I reached up, grabbed his finger and snapped it in two. It was pretty easy to do. I anchored two of my fingers behind his knuckle and pressed my thumb into the pad of his finger-tip. It made a sound similar to when you break a piece of kindling over your knee while building a campfire.

He screamed then, a long wailing moan.

"Molly," I repeated. "Where. Is. She."

"She hangs out at some place on the beach," the Candyman screamed, between sobs. Tears were streaming down his face and I realized he was wearing some kind of weird pancake makeup. It was streaking like worm trails through a patch of mud.

"On the beach," he added, "with a Haitian. A surfer." He almost screamed the last part. He was holding his finger which had already started to swell and turn blue.

I was about to follow up with another question, but something stopped me.

"Get away from him," a voice said to my right and sort of behind me.

I glanced over.

The black girl who'd been sitting next to Candyman was now leaning against the fence, a shiny revolver in her hand pointed at the ground. She held it with a casual, everyday expression. Loose in her hand. Like a set of car keys.

Good at following orders, I took a step back.

"Why did you do that to him?" she asked.

"He was being an asshole," I replied.

"What else is new?" she answered. "You do that to every jackass you run into?"

"No, just the ones who won't give me what I want."

She smiled then, a row of dynamite white

teeth, they practically shone like flawless diamonds.

"I like your style," she said. "Now get away from him and run along."

"What's your name?" I asked.

The gun slowly came up.

I raised my hands and backed away, then circled back to the Maverick.

For the first time since Margaret Hornor hired me, I felt good. After all, I thought, how hard could it be to find a Haitian surfer?

14

Surfers tend to stick together.

In some ways, it was a structured social club. They tended to recognize one another by experience, expertise and attitude.

I wasn't an accomplished surfer, but I'd learned the basics.

So in addition to working hard to wipe the memory of Candyman's orange ass from my memory, I swung into a gas station and filled up the Maverick's tank and headed back home.

Instead of hopping onto I-95, I stuck to the A1A, the narrow road that runs next to the ocean. It was slow going but I had the windows down and savored the warm ocean breeze.

Of course, by law you have to stop when beachgoers cross the street and I slowed down more than once to see the sun worshippers haul their load toward either the ocean or the parking lot.

It was interesting to note the difference in body posture. The ones headed toward the water were full of energy and even a little excited.

Going the other way they moved a lot slower. Relaxed. Sunburned or drunk. Or all three.

Eventually, I hit my cross street and turned away from the water, eventually getting back home.

I pulled into the driveway, got out and locked the car. Just as I was about to unlock the door, I saw a shadow fall across my window so I ducked and twisted to the right.

The tire iron was almost to my head before I caught the arm that held it.

Out of my crouch, I exploded into the chest of the big Florida Cracker whose hand I'd stabbed at Hammerhead's house. That hand was in a bandage, and the tire iron was in the other.

I had hooked his foot and he went down, hard, on his back which gave time for his companion, Squirrel, to stand there frozen.

This was not a man of action.

Too late, he decided to go for the gun inside his

denim jacket but by then, I'd use my momentum to carry me past Cracker and throw a straight right into Squirrel's mouth.

It was an awful blow, I'm not going to lie. There had been no need to employ any defense on my part, so I'd torqued my body and put everything behind it. A powerful piston of a blow with my fist, which was a size and a half bigger than most.

Squirrel's lips split like a ripe tomato, blood spraying and his upper teeth folded under my knuckles. His knees went out from under him and as he fell, I snatched the gun from his jacket, flipped it so I was holding the barrel, turned to see Cracker staggering to his feet and swung the gun sideways, hoping to connect the butt with the big man's temple.

I just missed, though, and instead, the protruding point of the gun's hammer sunk into Cracker's forehead and ripped a furrow all along his forehead from eyebrow to eyebrow. It was a really horrible sight because a giant flap of skin had broken loose and folded over his eyes, like some kind of disgusting flesh visor.

Blood poured down and he screamed, blinded and in the dark. Knowing there was plenty of time, I reached down and plucked the tire iron from his hand and bashed him over the head with it. This too, was done with no small amount of force. So much, in fact, that it was wedged into his skull and I had to yank it hard to get it back out. Once it was free I stepped back and swung it in a short, vicious arc, connecting with his jaw which came completely loose and left his face looking like a Picasso sketch.

He dropped like the giant sack of crap that he was, and landed right next to Squirrel.

I quickly pulled their bodies behind the Maverick, so they weren't visible from the street and then fished the keys from Cracker's pocket. His giant 4x4 had to be somewhere nearby. I walked down the driveway and up to the nearest intersection, but there was no sign of it, so I walked back the other way and over to the next block. Just as I was about to use the lock button to trigger the horn, I spotted it one more block over, via a glimpse between two of my neighbors' homes.

It was a bit surprising that he had used so much caution parking this far away from my house. The big Cracker hadn't acted like he put much thought into planning. If he wasn't dead, I would be sure to give him a compliment.

A quick unlock from the key fob and I hopped

into the driver's seat. It was odd to be sitting up so high. I immediately understood the attraction for a guy like my unconscious opponent. It made one feel powerful, almost superior, looking down on everyone. I keyed the ignition and from the stereo some country song about fried chicken and beer blasted out at me. I turned the stereo off, put the big vehicle into gear and drove to my house where I backed the truck into my driveway.

I lowered the tailgate, and checked my house-guests. Cracker was in bad shape. Either dead or a coma. It didn't concern me enough to check.

Squirrel was sort of coming to, so I nursed him gently back to sleep with the tire iron, then threw both of them into the truck bed. I raised the tail-gate, climbed back in and drove away from my house.

It took a little over twenty minutes to get into the worst neighborhood I could find. A nasty little stretch of West Palm Beach full of murderers, rapists and ex-convicts. My two companions would feel right at home, if they ever regained consciousness.

There was a deserted alley with a few rats skit-tering here and there, so I shut off the truck, left the key in the ignition, rolled the windows down and walked up to the nearest cross street. Using my phone, I fired up the Uber app and within three minutes an Arab woman in a Toyota Corolla picked me up.

The car smelled like cheap perfume and the penguin tank at the zoo.

God bless America.

15

Human blood and teeth on the driveway tended to drive down neighborhood property values. So even though the Maverick was already spotless, I pretended to wash it in order to clean up after my most inhospitable guests. I figured Squirrel was the one who'd leaked all over the place.

Some people just couldn't take a punch.

When that was done, I went inside, cleaned up and threw on a pair of board shorts, flip flops and a swim shirt.

Kicking the shit out of those two losers had made me hungry so I whipped together a quick sandwich using lavash flatbread, turkey and lettuce with a squirt of wasabi, followed with a big glass of iced tea.

Back outside I opened up the garage, revealing my other vehicle. This one was a 1971 International Harvester 4x4 Scout. IH was a company based in Illinois that used to make farm machinery and other vehicles. As far as I knew, it was either out of business or had sold to another company,

I'd had this baby rebuilt from the ground up by the same former client who'd done the Maverick. It had a custom teal paint job, with big oversized off-road wheels, and a killer sound system.

This one was customized for beach duty. It had a true jeep feel, totally exposed but everything was rubber and steel, easily cleaned with a garden hose. The upholstery was a custom job, too. A special blend of vinyl and polymer that felt like leather.

I backed the Scout out of the garage, and pulled the Maverick inside. From a wall, I grabbed my surfboard and slid it into the custom-made rack on the Scout.

After locking everything up, I steered the Scout back onto the road, and down to the beach.

The east coast of Florida isn't known as a great surfing spot. The waves are steady, but not huge. In the summer, the Gulf Stream pushes up from the south and the water is warm and calm. In the winter, the winds go the other way and the waves get bigger and the water colder.

Kite surfing is more popular than regular surfing, but there are still spots where surfers gather.

The main one near Delray Beach is a place the locals call Zuma, after the well-known Zuma Beach in California.

No one seems to know where the nickname came from, but most figure it was a California transplant who somehow made it stick. Whatever the case, the surfing spot wasn't crowded when I pulled the Scout into a rare available parking space along the A1A.

Hoisting my surfboard on my shoulder, I walked out onto the beach and down to the water. There were plenty of people already in place. There were multiple beach volleyball games going on, mostly guys shouting at each other over the boom box blasting some sort of rap hip-hop mashup.

A family was engaging in a fiery game of paddleball.

You had groups of people lounging on blankets, bottles of beer in hand, along with the occasional loner strumming a ukulele with an upturned hat looking for donations.

Fifty yards offshore were a half-dozen surfers, most just straddling their boards, waiting for the waves to pick up. I waded in, slid onto my board and paddled out next to them.

"Yo," I said to the nearest guy, a long-haired white guy covered with tribal tattoos. I wondered if his "tribe" was a suburb. Maybe the long, elaborate tribal tattoo on his arm stood for Pelican Sound Condominium complex, a Pulte home development.

"Hey bruh," he said.

"Has it been calm like this all day?" I asked.

"Nah, just died down ten minutes ago. Just a lull, I think."

I nodded and we watched a guy take on a small wave, he got to his feet and rode it briefly before flattening out onto the board and body surfing in.

"I heard there's some good waves up by Daytona," my tribal friend said. "My ex lives up there and she told me it's been gnarly for the last week or so."

"Never surfed up there," I said. "I go wherever my buddy says the waves are. He's the best Haitian surfer I've ever met."

The guy looked at me. "Shit. You mean Chief? That dude's crazy, man."

"Yeah, but he knows his waves."

"I haven't seen the Chief lately. He still up by Ocean Ridge?"

"Yeah, mostly."

My tribal surfer buddy shook his head. "I watched him kick some dude's ass at Doc's. Scary, man. I thought he was going to kill the guy."

"Don't mess with the Chief," I said. "Or you learn the hard way."

Suddenly, the wind changed and a nice roller came toward us.

"Yeah baby," my new friend said. He paddled hard and caught the wave, rode it toward the beach.

I caught the next one and let it carry me all the way onto shore where I picked up my surfboard, walked back to the street where I washed every-thing off at a shower kiosk and then stowed my board back on the Scout.

I fired her up, and headed north along the A1A, toward Ocean Ridge.

And the Chief.

16

Doc's is a legendary bar on the beach in Ocean Ridge, which is across the inter-coastal from Lake Worth. A decent stretch of sand, some good waves and a little bit of normalcy before those heading north on the A1A hit Palm Beach and the mega mansions.

Price of entry in Palm Beach is around four million or so.

For a fixer-upper.

Ocean Ridge is more down-to-earth. Its neighbor to the west, Lake Worth, is on its way back, striving for the hip vibes of Delray Beach. It's got a ways to go, especially when you consider the areas near the freeway.

I pulled the Scout into Doc's parking lot, made

sure my board was locked up and went inside, through the indoor bar area, out to the beachside bar. It's where all the action typically occurs.

Surfing, whether actually doing it or simply watching, always made me thirsty and I ordered a beer.

My table was facing the beach and I could see a half-dozen surfers trying to make the most of some pretty weak waves. When my beer came, I hoisted the cold bottle and took a nice long pull.

Mmm. Hit the spot. Something about surfing and beer that make them the perfect combination.

A little game of beach volleyball caught my eye because it was all-female and competitive. I'm no expert, but it looked to me like some pretty high-quality athleticism going on, and it was a pleasure to watch, on multiple levels.

Eventually, the game ended and some of the surfers came in from the water. None of them were black, but most were tanned a deep brown. Still, I knew I was looking for a Haitian, and none of them seemed to fit the description.

The waitress brought me another beer, without my asking which earned her a special place in my heart.

You just can't teach that stuff, I thought.

This one tasted even better than the first and I was beginning to think I might just have to call it quits for the day and spend the rest of my time here at Doc's, enjoying the sunset and maybe meeting a volleyball player.

That plan was interrupted, however, by the arrival of two people on the beach.

Actually, arrival is the wrong word.

They arrived in the sense that they came to my attention. However, it was their departure that precipitated the event. They had apparently been on a towel below the high water mark, not visible to me from the outdoor patio.

I put my beer down and leaned forward. The man was definitely black, big and had on board shorts, not that it means anything down here in Florida. Everybody wears them, surfers or not.

The girl was behind him and I stood, threw a twenty on the table and walked out to the edge of the sand where I waited to see which way they would go. There was the main parking area just behind the bar, and then there was some off-street parking, which is where the couple headed.

As quickly as I could, I trotted around to the Scout, climbed in and fired up the engine. I pulled out onto the street, and saw the girl getting into the front passenger side of a Mercedes-Benz G-Wagon, while the black guy got into the other side.

Even though the view had been a quick glimpse, there was no doubt in my mind.

I had found Molly.

17

The Benz G-Wagon is my favorite vehicle to tail.

It's just so easy.

The damn thing is like a giant box on wheels, sitting up higher than just about everything except the swamp truck 4x4s with the jacked-up chassis.

Even better, the Chief's G-Wagon was sporting a clearly custom color: silver with flecks of gold. As it moved through traffic, I felt like I was following a float in the Macy's Thanksgiving Day parade.

Eventually, we crossed over the intercoastal onto the A1A and the G-Wagon pulled into a gated compound. Over the entrance, I saw a three-story ode to modern beach architecture. It was cement block painted a stark white, with balconies and a circular drive that wound around a fountain. The fountain's central figure was a naked woman. I could've been wrong, but it looked like the sculpture's figure was wearing a gold chain.

Unable to linger and not willing to pull over to the side of the road to gawk, I drove on, catching a quick glimpse of Molly exiting the passenger side of the G-Wagon.

I drove on, then turned off onto the next block and made my way back past the compound.

Even from the road, I could see the impressive security features, including a large man with a walkie talkie stationed near the front door.

At this point, my mission had been to locate Molly and at least make sure she was alive.

Mission accomplished.

For it to transition to a hostage rescue operation I would have to contact my client. However, it didn't appear to me that Molly was being held against her will. Then again, I hadn't seen her up close and personal.

Maybe the Chief had her doped up on drugs and was leading her around like a pet zombie.

I kind of doubted it, but I'd seen stranger things.

The situation called for more surveillance,

most likely, and maybe even a call to the cops, depending on what my client wanted.

Once I crossed the bridge, I plugged my phone into my hands-free calling system I'd had custom installed in the Scout and dialed up Margaret Hornor.

She wasn't available so I left a message and headed back home.

My home gym in the garage was calling me, but so was the pool. I decided to split the difference with a short workout – what's the expression 'anything is good, more is better' – and a dive into the pool. I floated around for awhile, then got out and filled a bucket with three beers and some ice, then slipped back into the water.

I have an inflatable lounge chair I can float in so I slithered into it and put my head back, let the soft breeze nudge me in different directions as I drank my beer. Around me, I could hear the subtle background music of the neighborhood. A car passing on the street behind my house. A dog yapped in the distance, probably the little old lady's Yorkie I saw from time to time. Cinnamon was her name. The dog, not the old lady.

A different tone reached my ear. I took a drink of beer and listened to the soft murmur of an engine. It had depth to it. Not like the big growl of a truck. No, this was the sound of a good motor.

And then it shut off.

There were always weapons nearby, I'd made sure of that shortly after buying the place.

Something told me I didn't need them, though.

So I drank. And waited.

Eventually, I heard the unmistakable echo of a woman's sandals walking up my driveway.

I shifted slightly, making the floating lounge chair face my back gate and the entrance to the pool.

Margaret Hornor appeared.

She had on a sundress, white, with silver aviators sporting gray lenses. A small clutch was in one hand and her cell phone in the other.

"I got your message," she said.

"I can see that."

While I've always said I'm not much to look at, I will admit that there is a certain quality to my physique that occasionally attracts attention. Whether it was the width of my shoulders, the depth of my chest, or simply the surprising appearance of me in the water, Margaret Hornor spent a fair amount of time staring at me.

"Thought I'd pop by for your report rather than playing phone tag," she said.

I nodded.

"Did I give you my address?"

She smiled. "Private investigators aren't the only ones who can do a little detective work."

Now it was my turn to grin.

"Why don't you grab something to drink from the fridge over there and meet me poolside? I'll tell you what I know."

She ignored me and came directly to the edge of the pool. She glanced down at me and I could see twin reflections of myself in the lenses of her sunglasses.

Man, I looked really relaxed.

"I just want to know if she's okay."

"Yes, of course," I said. "I mentioned that in my message."

"Thank God," she said, her shoulders sagging inward. "I didn't listen to your message."

"She's fine. Hanging out on the beach with a surfer nicknamed the Chief."

"Of course," Margaret said. "You know what? I will take that drink."

I watched her walk over to my outdoor kitchen area and bar. I couldn't tell if she was depressed, angry, sad or happy by the news. Maybe it was a combination of all of them.

She looked especially good when she reached down into my fridge for a beer. The shape was quite intriguing.

Something told me she was wearing a bikini under that sundress.

Or maybe nothing at all.

18

"Is this how you give all of your client updates?" she asked, taking a seat in a rattan chair with a white cushion at the edge of the pool. She crossed her long, tanned legs, and sipped from a beer.

"What, it isn't casual Friday?"

I slid off the chair into the water, walked to the shallow end and got out. I wrapped a towel around my waist and sat in the chair next to her.

"I think it's casual Friday every day for you, am I right?" she asked.

"More often than not," I said.

"So why don't you start at the beginning?"

That's what I did, starting with my contact, tracing the lead to a dealer, and then following that to the Chief. I left out the part about the Florida Cracker and Squirrel.

"Well, I'm disappointed, but certainly not surprised," Margaret said.

"About which part?"

She signed. "All of it, really."

I nodded. Drugs usually don't have a lot of Hallmark moments.

"The Chief?" she asked. "What the hell kind of name is that?"

"He's a surfer, they always have nicknames," I answered. "Supposedly he's Haitian, but I'm not so sure. Maybe he's Native American. Or Samoan."

Margaret considered that. The sun was sinking faster now and it cast a bronze glow over her smooth skin. She must have caught me looking at her because when she held out her empty, there was a little bit of a smirk on her face.

"Mind if I do a few laps while you refresh my drink?" she asked.

"Since you are my guest, yes, be my guest." Not the smoothest line but she laughed, went to the edge of the pool and crossed her arms in front of her, grabbed the bottom of her cover up and pulled it off in one smooth motion.

Wow.

Very nice.

Suddenly, I realized I was supposed to be getting her drink so I turned just as she jumped into the water. I heard splashing and glanced back, seeing her arms knifing through the water.

Yep, definitely an athlete. A swimmer.

I brought her drink back to the table and watched as she cut through the water with liquid precision and supple power. After maybe twenty laps she smoothly stood and walked up the steps to the pool deck. She shook her head, wrapped a towel around herself and joined me in the seating area. She was breathing a little quickly, but something told me she was in such good shape that would hardly qualify as a warm-up.

"Was that a warm-up?" I asked.

She raised an eyebrow at me over the glass in her hand.

"Well, that depends on you, doesn't it?"

Now it was my turn to seek a little extra oxygen.

"How about a tour?" I asked, nodding my head toward the house.

"I was going to ask for one."

We went inside and I gave her the showing, but I knew she wasn't all that interested.

Finally, I realized we weren't exactly twenty-year-olds.

"You look a little cold," I said, as I moved in and took her in my arms.

Actually, she was anything but.

Warm to the touch.

My lips found hers and we kept them together as I pulled her into the bedroom.

19

They say that once an athlete, always an athlete.

Margaret Hornor amply proved that several times over the course of the night.

If there's a better way to start the day than with physical exertion between the sheets with my new client, I don't have any idea what that might be. An omelet with Jesus? Bloody Marys with the Dali Lama?

I swung out of bed and walked to the kitchen. There was a bit of soreness from the night's acrobatics. In fact, maybe I had misjudged my guest's sporting background and rather than swimming she had been a gymnastics star.

I made a full pot of coffee because I figured we

were both going to need it, considering how little sleep we actually enjoyed.

Just then, I felt arms circle my waist and a chin rest on my shoulder.

"Thanks for making the coffee," she said. "And for everything else."

We each took a cup and sat at my little kitchen table, with sheepish grins on our faces.

Yes, it had been that much fun.

My kitchen was filled with sun and centered with a circular table and chairs.

It was a vintage modern set. The two chairs were surprisingly comfortable, even though they looked like they would be anything but.

"So now what?" she asked. And then, after a pause, "In terms of Molly, I mean."

"That's up to you," I said. "You mentioned the police were involved before so I think we should turn it over to them now that we know where she is. They're probably best equipped to handle the next step. If they have to break into the Chief's compound, at least they've got a SWAT team who could handle it. And they might need it."

I have to admit that's not really what I wanted to do. I wanted to keep working on the case because I was intrigued by Margaret Hornor.

Okay, intrigued was a bullshit word.

This woman was hotter than the sand at noon in August, and I had suddenly developed a taste for that heat.

But I'm a responsible businessman.

Which was why I suggested turning it over to Delray Beach's finest.

"Nope. Sorry, nope," she said. "No police. I don't want them involved."

"Wait a minute, I thought you had already talked to the police."

She glanced out my kitchen window which looked out onto the pool. It was a cool sheet of jade.

"They were initially involved," she said. "But I just talked to them. I didn't actually file a missing persons report." She took a deep breath and soldiered on. "Look, the situation is a little more complicated than I initially made it out to be."

"Complicated how?" I asked, even though I had a fairly good idea of what was about to come.

"Let's just say Molly's father isn't completely out of the picture. See, he was an investment banker and he played pretty fast and loose with his clients' money and never really came clean with it."

"Like a Bernie Madoff kind of thing?" I asked, referencing the investment "advisor" who swindled celebrities out of hundreds of millions of dollars through a Ponzi scheme.

She seemed to be at a loss for words, which I took as a big 'yes.'

"So, what's the deal?" I asked. "Is he on the run?"

She spread her hands wide. "No, no, no. No. He's not on the run, as you say. It's just that, as the situation stands, I don't want to involve the police. It would complicate things."

I was neither surprised nor disappointed. Clients never want to share everything at once. It usually arrives in bits and pieces like debris from a shipwreck washing up on the beach.

Which was fine with me. I wasn't going to start investigating her husband. And I certainly didn't want to get mixed up in a case for which I hadn't been hired. All of which lead me to my next question.

"What do you want to do?"

She gave a little smile to me, flashed the beautiful blue eyes that had blazed with so much intensity in the dim light of my bedroom.

"First, I want to go back into the bedroom with you and welcome the day properly."

She took a drink of her coffee, then set down the empty cup. She looked out toward the pool and then back at me, meeting my gaze with frank honesty.

"And then I want you to bring my Molly home."

20

E ventually we said goodbye.

However, before she left, Margaret had agreed to extend my contract at double my normal rate, after I had been clear about the difficulties I would face with the Chief's compound and its extensive security. It would just be me, no backup, no SWAT team, no partner.

Once Margaret left, I showered, dressed, locked the house up and drove to the office.

There, I fired up the desktop computer and performed some clerical duties that come with running a business like mine. Not a lot of paper-work, certainly enough to merit an hour or two a week, though.

I had thought about hiring a secretary at one

point, but privacy is more important to me than delegation of duties. I'd rather work a couple more hours a day than open up my dealings to anyone.

After that, I took lunch out on my balcony that overlooked Delray Beach and thought about next steps.

Although I had told my client there wouldn't be any backup available to me, in the back of my mind I thought Delary Beach Police Officer Paula Barbieri might be of some assistance.

She and I had been playing a game of teasing without pleasing for a couple of years.

I had first bumped into her on a case where a local lifeguard had gone missing. The family and the police couldn't find him so his girlfriend hired me.

It turned out he had decided to move to Little Havana outside Miami and was working as a male prostitute. It brought new meaning to the term 'buddy system.'

I shot Barbieri a text.

"How does a little Mexican sound?" I asked.

Minutes later, she responded, "Like Herve Villechaize? If that's the case, he sounds like *the plane, boss, the plane!*"

"Cute, but I think he was French," I pointed out.

"How the hell would you know that?"

"Probably a trivia question," I said. "So, how about El Matador at noon? My client is buying."

I added the last part just to give her fair warning that this was going to be more than just a flirting meal.

Hey, don't get me wrong. There would be plenty of that.

But I wanted to let her know that there would actually be a little bit of business to do, in and around the mating dance.

Back I went to work on the computer fielding a few email inquiries and matching purchase orders with invoices.

My clientele was fairly exclusive. Which meant there was no real need or desire on my part to advertise. All of my business was word-of-mouth, I didn't have business cards or bus signs or flyers.

And if you knew how to contact me you probably already knew what I was capable of and the kinds of services I offered.

In the back of my office I had a very small but highly secure armory.

Inside was a small selection of handguns, some

knives, ammunition and even a slim-fitting Kevlar vest.

It had been at least a week or two since I'd done the mandatory cleaning of the guns, so I spent the next hour before my meeting with Barbieri taking apart all my guns. The Sig Sauer, Glock, Colt 1911, Ruger .357.

After the cleaning and oiling was done, I reassembled them, and locked them all up, except for the ones I was bringing with me.

Since I wasn't quite sure how the day was going to go, I strapped a small LCR lightweight concealed carry to my ankle.

And I put the Colt .45 1911 in the holster on my belt, which I covered with a loose-fitting shirt. Tommy Bahama. Hey, don't judge me. When you live in Florida near the beach, it pays to look like you live near the beach in Florida. Especially if you're going to observe someone who probably doesn't want any extra attention.

With that all set I locked up the office, went down to the Maverick, started her up and found my way to el Matador, a little Mexican place just north of downtown Delray on a quiet little street tucked away between an art gallery and a pool cleaning supply service.

Since I was the one who was going to make a request of the other, I made sure to arrive early, and nab a little table in the back. I ordered chips and guacamole, salsa and bottled water with fresh limes.

The décor was surprisingly elaborate. A lot of Mexican paintings, sombreros, masks from the Yucatan on the wall and authentic Mexican music playing through a couple of tinny speakers.

The owner's name was Flora Alvarez and I knew her well. She'd been in Florida for nearly 30 years and although I wasn't sure if she was legal or not, all of her food was made from scratch and in my opinion, was the best Mexican cuisine on the east coast of Florida.

"Senor Wade," she said. "Will your girlfriend be joining you?" she said, nodding toward the food and water I'd already ordered.

"Which one?"

She smiled.

"When are you going to get married, Mr. Carver?"

"I don't know, Flora. I do know that I will get married in the morning, though."

"And why is that?"

"Because if it doesn't work out I don't want to ruin a whole day."

She laughed a nice, deep belly laugh and just then Barbieri spoke from behind her.

"Don't get fooled by him, Flora. He's a bad, bad man." She slid into the seat across from me, her leather gun belt creaking with the motion. She looked good, even with her hair pulled back and very little makeup. Her skin was beautiful, a golden light brown that looked like silk.

"Ah, Miss Paula," Flora said. "So good to see the two of you together again. You would make beautiful babies. How is that project coming along?"

Barbieri rolled her big brown eyes.

"Procreating with this guy would be a really bad idea," she said. "One Carver does enough damage around here. Could you imagine what a herd of them would do?"

I laughed, appreciating the reference to me as a form of cattle.

"The usual, por favor," I said to Flora, who left and Barbieri smiled at me.

"Oh, you would like that, wouldn't you?" she asked. "I could just imagine your enthusiasm in trying to knock me up."

"Only one way to find out, baby," I said. "So what's shaking down at the shop?"

Barbieri was always good for a cop story or two.

"We found a tourist this morning passed out on the beach. He had an empty bottle of tequila next to him. He'd been in the sun all day passed out and his back was sunburned to almost third degree burns. It looked like at some point maybe some of his friends had recognized that he was getting painfully sunburned."

Flora put the first of our food on the table, but Barbieri kept going.

"So instead of helping him, you know, maybe waking him up, or slathering sunblock on him, they decided to do something else."

She unfolded her napkin and placed it on her lap,

"They squirted limes all over him, like he was a piece of roasting meat," she said.

"Lime really does go with just about anything," I pointed out. "I especially like it over jicama."

We dug into our food then. 'The usual' was a steady stream of small, delicious tacos with everything from chicken to chorizo to shrimp to fire-roasted poblano peppers.

We tore into them and talk subsided.

"So what do I owe this expensive meal to?" Barbieri asked me, a touch of guacamole in the corner of her mouth. Damn, it was sexy.

I washed down the last of a lobster taco, took a drink of my water, smiled at her and asked, "What do you know about the Chief?"

"My Chief?"

I shook my head.

"Oh, you mean the nasty surfer dude who deals drugs and is rumored to be linked with a cartel?"

"Yeah, that one."

"All I know is a delicate flower like you is no match for him."

21

After lunch, Barbieri and I went back to my office where we made mad, passionate love. Okay, kidding. Not at all. Actually what happened was she boxed up the rest of her meal (I had no leftovers as usual) and we parted ways. The only thing she gave me was a promise that she would nose around a little bit among her fellow cops and see if there was any information on the Chief.

Usually, cops aren't very talkative but I figured among the boys in blue, there would be more than one or two who would love to have a conversation with Barbieri.

Her talent was always on full display.

On my way out, I grabbed a toothpick, put it in the corner of my mouth and climbed into the Maverick. The thing I wanted to do now was get a feel for the Chief, see if there was any kind of routine. Trouble was, the Maverick wasn't a great vehicle to use. There was a buddy of mine who drove a Toyota Corolla, beige, that I called the world's most invisible car. Sometimes I would let him use the Maverick so I could borrow the Corolla for surveillance.

But I was feeling a little impatient, so I drove back to the area on the beach where I'd spotted the Chief and Molly before, and parked in a spot at the ass-end of the lot, well away from anyone who might see me approaching.

After locking up the car, I made my way to the beach, past the surfing area where only one guy was plying his trade in the water. A skinny white guy covered in tats.

From there, I walked across the boardwalk back to the street, and followed the sidewalk toward the Chief's place.

It wasn't a long walk, but the sun was out and I broke a sweat. A small one. Nothing wrong with that. In fact, it felt good. Although I worked out a lot in my home gym in the garage, I preferred exercising outdoors. The sun felt good, and I'd spent plenty of long winters in Michigan, enough to appreciate the warmth of a sunny day, even if they arrived one after the other.

The street bordered the beach, and I frequently had to skirt around people either arriving or departing, dragging their beach chairs, umbrellas and coolers. When I had tailed the Chief and Molly previously, I could have sworn I had seen a café or ice cream shop or something not far from his compound.

Finally, I spotted it.

Flavio's Coffee & Cream. A combination coffee and ice cream shop with outdoor seating. The outdoor tables and chairs were the only things I was really interested in, but I went inside and got a tall coffee, just so I could sit outside and watch the Chief's driveway.

My vantage point was the last spot of retail before the road turned north, demarcating the commercial zone from the residential. The Chief's compound was the third one, and certainly overlooked the beach, with sweeping ocean views.

There was a family seated behind me, pasty white with New Jersey accents. The parents were bickering with each other, the kids were silent. Ah, a family vacation.

My secret hope was that the Chief would pull out of his compound in his G-Wagon and cruise down to his surf spot. From here, it would be nearly impossible to miss him. Of course, if he was truly loaded with money and living the gangster life, he would have more than one car. Probably a Bentley. Maybe an Italian, too. Ferrari or Lamborghini. I immediately pictured the Chief as a Lambo guy. The Ferrari would be too classic for him.

The fighting family eventually moved on, and I found my coffee empty and I knew I definitely didn't want another one. I threw the empty into the garbage can outside the café and walked back to the beach, cruised past the lone surfer and then turned and walked back.

It was at about the halfway point between the beach and the Chief's compound when the Rolls-Royce cruised past me. It was driving slowly and even though the windows were tinted, the windshield wasn't, because it's illegal to do so.

The clear view allowed me to get a good look at the passenger.

It was a beautiful young white woman.

Molly.

The driver was unmistakable.

The Chief.

And he was looking right at me.

22

The great thing about Florida beach towns are the brazen attempts of retailers to sell the cheapest, flimsiest crap to desperate tourists for exorbitant sums. A little plastic beach chair that would be overpriced for ninety-nine cents at a dollar store in Indiana? Yeah, we're going to let you have that for $14.99.

To think that the tourists from Indiana weren't going to have any of that would be foolish, because the stores seemed to be booming with the kind of foot traffic (or flip-flop traffic) that would be the envy of every H&M on the planet.

It wasn't too much trouble to duck into one of them, buy a Florida Gator T-shirt and a weird kind of country music cowboy hat made out of a cross between plastic and cardboard. I looked like Toby Keith if he was on Skid Row.

Nevertheless, since the Chief had gotten a good look at me, I figured it might be better to make a little change to my appearance. I had an idea in the back of my mind and I was hoping it would work.

Back I went to the beach, my hat pulled low and my body set to relax mode. There was a lazy quality to tourists on the beach, even the Type-A personalities. My strategy was to look like a guy half-interested in collecting seashells and half-interested in ogling women in bikinis. It was a stretch, I know, but I'm a method actor and take my craft very seriously.

By the time I made it up to the group of surfers lounging by the best of the waves, the wind had picked up a bit, which was perfect.

It was almost like a cliché. The first people on beach towels was a group of four who were some of the most sickly white people I'd ever seen. All looking like they just got out of juvie. Lots of piercings and big gnarly tattoos everywhere.

Beyond them, a guy who was way too old sat on a towel playing a clunky ukulele and singing some kind of song that sounded more like a dying sea mammal than anything else.

The crazy bastard was selling cassette tapes of his music.

Cassette tapes!

He would have made more money selling a cassette *player* than his jive ass tapes. Vintage always sells better.

The wind picked up steam and it was almost like the fates were intervening. Because as the waves picked up, several of the surfers from the large group beyond the horrible ukulele player picked up the boards and dashed toward the water.

The last in line was the Chief.

He was even bigger and more impressive in person. A little shorter than my 6'3" but a whole lot wider. He picked the board up one-handed which was an impressive feat in and of itself, and trotted toward the water with it balanced on his shoulder.

All of which left Molly without her companion sitting in an anti-gravity chaise lounge. There was another young woman next to her, and a third sitting a few yards back, smoking a cigarette.

It was now or never.

"Molly?" I asked as I approached.

She glanced over at me, her eyes hidden

behind sunglasses. The big round kind, tortoise shell. But even with the eyewear, I could see the resemblance with Margaret. Younger, not as tall, but with the same kind of poise.

"You *were* following us," she said, a small grin on her face.

No point in denying it. "Your Mom wants me to bring you home. How about we go?"

She laughed, a mirthless exhalation of breath and tone if there ever was one.

"You actually *are* as dumb as you look," she said.

The girl in back with the cigarette had disappeared, and now she re-emerged with two big guys in black shirts, clearly not dressed for the beach.

"Enlighten me," I said.

"Are you talking to my woman, bro?" the voice came from behind me, and I knew without turning the Chief had caught a wave in as soon as he'd seen me approach Molly.

Now I was surrounded by three large men. I figured the Chief wasn't armed, maybe a knife inside his suit, but the two guys were.

"Take my advice and run along and tell Margaret to save what's left of her dwindling money," Molly said. "It's your healthiest option."

"You look familiar to me," the Chief said.

His face was dripping with saltwater and he stepped closer to me. I was ready if we were going to go toe-to-toe, but I could tell that wasn't his plan.

"Do you have a sister?" he asked me.

23

There was a brief moment when the first scenario played out in my mind. It was the one I really wanted to do, because the Chief's comment about my sister was said with a certain edge.

He knew something.

It triggered an urge in me to choke the information out of him on the spot. But I knew it wasn't the time or the place.

It still played out in my head, though. The scenario involved knocking out the Chief with an elbow to his jaw, shooting both of the armed security men and hoisting Molly over my shoulder and executing a fireman's carry all the way back to my car.

Then I would return to the beach and torture the Chief until he gave me the information about my sister I needed.

As you might imagine, I thought better.

"No, I'm an only child," I said. "That's why I'm so spoiled. I'm used to getting my own way and being the center of attention."

There was no response. A seagull flew overhead, thought better about dive bombing this particular group for scraps of soggy sandwich bread, and moved on.

"Molly doesn't have that experience," I continued. "Her sister goes to Harvard and here she is hanging out on the beach with a bunch of drug-dealing losers."

Molly sat up a little straighter. "That's a funny observation coming from a guy who probably just slept with a woman whose husband is a criminal and she isn't much better. In fact, she's probably worse than he is."

By now the armed guards in their black T-shirts had come even closer and I could see the thought in their eyes about trying to outflank me on the beach. That would be a bad thing for me. I took a step back gave a little half salute to Molly and turned to the Chief.

"You and I will be talking a little bit later."

"Looking forward to it," he said.

I walked away and threw my ridiculous hat onto the chair of a tourist who was probably splashing around in the water like a beached pilot whale with faulty navigation.

The Florida Gators T-shirt came off and I tossed it near the outdoor showers for some home-less person to use. Just because you don't have a permanent address doesn't mean you can't root for the home team.

When I got back to the Maverick I keyed the ignition and hit the road, planning to go to my office and do some more research on Margaret Hornor and her husband. If he was a big finance guy, I could probably find something on the Inter-net. Molly's comment had gotten my wheels turning and I wanted more information.

About a block away from the office my phone buzzed. I glanced down and saw that Barbieri had texted me a PDF which was attached. After parking in my spot at the office, I locked up the Maverick and forwarded the text to my email. Once upstairs and at my desk, I opened the email, downloaded the file and printed it off.

It was the Chief's rap sheet. As I suspected he

wasn't actually Haitian, he was Jamaican. His father was from Jamaica and his mother was Samoan, which explained the tribal tattoos.

His criminal history was a perfect example of escalation. Starting with truancy and other juvenile crimes like shoplifting, trespassing and petty theft it then graduated to grand theft auto, assault, battery, and possession.

He'd done a couple of short stints in jail but it looked like he'd evaded the cops for at least a few years now.

In the file Barbieri sent me there was a hint that he was linked to a cartel in South America but any information on that was sketchy. But it didn't take a genius to realize that a piece of real estate like he had on the beach would easily go for a couple million. And then throw in the G-Wagon, the Rolls-Royce and you knew that he was raking in some big money.

After hitting the end of my research leads on the Chief, I decided to turn to Margaret Hornor and her supposed husband/financier.

A lot of Google searching didn't turn up anything mainly because I didn't know the husband's first name, so I focused my search on Margaret and was able to find an entry from four years earlier where she had hyphenated her last name.

I then entered that into Google and learned that she had called herself Margaret Hornor-Boswell.

So then I searched under the name Margaret Hornor-Boswell and found her linked to a man named John Boswell. There were multiple entries. Most of them in the form of social photographs with captions and charity events, yacht races and fundraising auctions.

Curious now, I used the image search and typed in "John Boswell."

Immediately several rows of photographs appeared, most of them being head shots of John Boswell from corporate websites that clearly dealt with investments.

On the fourth row of photographs there was a picture of John Boswell with a younger, even better-looking Margaret Hornor.

So now I knew what the shady money man looked like. That was a good thing because my security system alerted me to somebody at the door and when I checked the camera, I had a pleasant little surprise.

John Boswell's face filled my screen.

24

Knowing what was about to come I opened the door and he charged in like a blitzing linebacker.

The most important thing to me at that point was to make sure he didn't crash into my desk or my computer or any of my furniture. So I let him tackle me but in the process I steered him over toward an open area in front of my visitor chairs.

It was a simple move to let him bring me down but I slid to the side as we fell and when we hit the ground, I immediately slipped on top of him and employed a rear naked chokehold.

His cologne was probably Hugo Boss. He was a big guy, had possibly played middle linebacker on some small college football team twenty years ago.

There was still muscle but it was buried under fat and now on top I could see the side of his face was flushed red.

Probably not from the exertion.

From the brief glimpse I'd gotten, this guy looked like he worked hard and played even harder.

My chokehold was tight and he would go limp in less than 60 seconds unless he tapped out. But that required a certain knowledge of mixed martial arts and he didn't do it.

I had to grudgingly admire him for that.

When he finally went limp I let go and dug his wallet and phone out of his pocket and stood over him.

John Boswell, in the ample flesh.

His driver's license was from California, so at least Margaret wasn't lying about that. His iPhone was locked but I knelt down, grabbed his thumb and pressed it into the touchpad until the screen unlocked.

As the screen came to life, I let go of his meaty hand and it dropped to the floor where it landed with a smack.

I scrolled through his messages, most of them were from Margaret. Clearly, they still had some kind of a relationship. He was asking her all kinds of questions and she was being vague in her answers. I also saw that he had sent a bunch of text messages to Molly, all of which she had ignored.

However, I took advantage of the situation to write down Molly's cell phone number along with Margaret's, which was different from the one I had. No big surprise there.

Boswell started to move a little so I ducked into my little kitchen and got him a bottled water. People have told me that getting choked out makes you thirsty. A little tough on the windpipe, after all.

I leaned against the edge of my reception desk and waited for the big man to come to.

Finally, he rolled over and opened his eyes.

"What happened?" he asked.

"You made a clumsy tackle, I choked you out, sodomized you, and then waited for you to wake up."

His face turned red until he realized I wasn't telling the truth. He even reached down and checked if his pants were still in the proper position. It made me laugh a little bit.

"What's so funny?"

"Your family's dysfunction," I answered. "Your daughter won't talk to you, your wife won't give you a straight answer, and they both think you're some kind of pathetic white-collar criminal. What are your holiday meals like?"

He sat up, seemed fascinated by his leather shoes. Gucci, if I had to guess.

"Lonely," he said.

It surprised me. I thought for sure he would be a blowhard, defensive jackass. Maybe getting knocked out had humbled him.

He glanced at the water bottle in my hand and I tossed it to him. He tried to catch it but it went through his hands and thumped against his chest, then fell into his lap. Foggy brain from a lack of oxygen. He would recover.

He retrieved it, twisted off the cap and took a long drink. Seemingly more focused now, he glanced over at my visitor's chair, got to his knees, then stood and dropped into the chair.

For a moment, we both just looked at each other.

"Why don't you tell me why you're here?" I asked. "And spare me the bullshit. I already know too much."

Not exactly true. There was still quite a bit I didn't know. But the more he thought I knew, the less he would try to lie to me.

"What do you think? I'm going to let some meathead I don't know start messing around with my family?" he barked at me. "Sleeping with my ex? Chasing after my daughter?"

"Little late to be going for Father-of-the-Year, isn't it?"

"Screw you, pal."

He drank from his water. I saw eyes glance down and I knew he was gauging the distance between us, getting ready for another charge.

"Don't even think about it, Boswell," I said. "I was pretty kind just choking you out. I could have done some real damage. I'd hate to knock out all of those professionally bleached teeth and I'd hate to have to sweep up your veneers from my floor."

When he'd spoken, I could tell he'd had them done. It looked like he'd maybe even done some face-tucking here and there. South Florida was the capital of plastic surgery, more so than Los Angeles. At least Los Angeles tried to keep it somewhat dignified. Down here, you saw women everywhere with hideous masks. I mean, how much worse could their real faces look?

"You're an asshole," he said.

"And you're avoiding the issue," I said. "What, did Margaret tell you she hired me? Or are you one of those guys who follows his wife around and hides in the bushes?"

"From what I heard, you're the one hiding in my wife's bush," he said with a sneer.

At that moment, I decided that I really, really disliked John Boswell.

"You know what? I changed my mind, why don't you take another run at me?" I said, getting to my feet.

He practically shrank back into my visitor's chair.

"Look, look, I didn't mean that," he said. "I don't give a flying crap what Margaret does with her life anymore. I'm just trying to get her to stay the hell out of my business, you know what I mean? She's the frickin' devil, man! Don't you see that? I mean, I don't love her anymore–"

Suddenly, he stopped, and the pained expression on his face morphed into something else. It started with his chin and lower lip. They were practically quivering. And then, right before my eyes, his whole face turned up and he burst into the most riotous fit of laughter imaginable. He laughed and laughed, shaking so hard that he started holding his midsection.

"I'm sorry, I thought I could do it," he said. His laughing subsided, and he wiped the tears from his face, but then he had an aftershock, and it all started again, not quite as vigorous. Finally, that one passed.

"Are you done now?" I asked.

He let out a long exhalation of breath.

"Yeah, I think so."

"Care to fill me in?"

Boswell tossed me the water bottle, now empty and got to his feet.

"You're a smart guy, you figure it out," he answered.

He changed his mind when I slid from the edge of the desk and put myself between him and my door.

There was a mixture of fear and rebellion in his eyes. He was scared of me all right, but he still had some fight left in him. Easy way to take care of that.

I slapped him.

It was an easy blow, from the hip, open palm. The crack was loud, and Boswell's head snapped to the side.

It probably hurt a little.

But it damaged his pride even more.

No man on God's green earth wants to get bitch-slapped by another man.

When he faced me, there was still fear in his eyes, but now it was joined by shame, anguish and hurt feelings. The rebellion was gone.

"Margaret is my ex-wife, that's true. But Molly's not my daughter," Boswell said. "If you looked at my phone, you saw messages to Molly. I wasn't trying to reconnect with her. That's not what I was doing at all."

"Then what were you doing?"

"I was trying to warn her."

"Warn her?" I asked. "About me?"

He shook his head. "No, not you. Margaret. And Molly's real father. They're trying to get at the trust fund I provided her. That's the con, do you get it now?"

Whether or not I believed him wasn't the point. I understood the game he had just outlined.

"Who's her real father?" I asked.

He started laughing again and I made like I was going to slap him. He stopped and looked at me.

Shrugged his shoulders in an expression of hopelessness.

"Some loser called the Candyman."

25

I'm not going to lie, my pride was hurt.

The Candyman?

How incredibly disappointing. I could picture him now, flabby and white with tight orange shorts.

He also had a broken finger that was still probably healing, thanks to me. At the same time, I realized he'd held out on me, even though he'd looked scared shitless.

Still, it was very difficult to reconcile Margaret Hornor with that Orange-Shorted Nightmare.

Margaret Hornor was impeccable looking but her taste in men was apparently not held to the same standard. And now I had to include myself in that equation. It was difficult for me to even imagine Margaret Hornor and that pancake-makeup-wearing piece of crap I had rousted by the pool at the Oasis apartment building.

Jesus Christ in a sidecar.

Look, I'm not saying I've got the biggest ego in the world, but I consider that a low blow.

After Boswell left, I locked up the office and went home. When I got inside I could still smell Margaret Hornor. And instead of it being a delight, a titillating reminder of what had gone on in my house and mostly in my bedroom, it left me slightly aghast.

Shit.

I decided to work out my frustrations in the garage. I had a heavy bag and a speed bag and I punched and kicked and lifted weights, working up a sweat that splattered all over the gray, cement floor. It looked like a crime scene by the time I was done with my workout.

After that, a quick dip in the pool, a shower, a fast meal of mostly protein in the form of grilled steak and a few sliced jalapenos, and then I put on my gear.

The Colt 1911 went into its holster, my little snub-nosed Ruger strapped to my ankle, and into my pocket went my assisted-opening knife. Sort of like a switchblade, but legal.

Back in the Maverick, I cruised down to the Oasis, and parked in the same spot I'd used during my first visit.

From my earlier trip to the Oasis, I remembered the Carrot Cake Lady referring to the Candyman as the "weirdo in unit ii." She'd also mentioned that he was almost always by the pool.

The pool seemed like the best place to start, however, a leisurely walk past it revealed no one was in the mood for the sun or swimming.

Unit ii was a corner apartment and I walked past it. The windows were dark and it appeared no one was home.

However, I also remembered his black girl-friend, all sinewy muscle and how she held that shiny revolver so casually by her side. Not a woman to be trifled with.

So I stood and pretended to make a phone call while listening for any movement inside the Candyman's unit. There was nothing, so I quickly withdrew my lock pick from a hidden slot in my belt, jimmied the front door and stepped inside.

When the door opened, a little bit of ambient light came in and I saw the apartment's main room was empty. It wasn't much. A couch, a cheap kitchen table and a ten-year-old television on a sagging stand made of plywood.

I shut the door and the apartment went dark.

With my Colt in hand, I checked the bedroom, bathroom and the closet. All empty.

Now it was time to find the drugs. It didn't take long. His main stash was taped to the bottom of the toilet's reservoir lid.

I gave the Candyman a failing grade for creativity. That's the first place anyone would look.

Just to make sure there weren't any other goodies, I checked the closet, under the bed and between the mattresses. Nothing. After a search of any suspicious patches of carpet that might be hiding a compartment, as well as loose ceiling tiles, the result was the same.

Still, from the stash in the toilet I saw there was enough white powder to put the jackass in prison for quite awhile, assuming he had priors, which I was confident he did.

Now, there was nothing to do but wait. I took a chair that didn't smell as bad as the rest of the place, and started counting the minutes.

I'm great at waiting. Extreme patience is one of my better qualities.

The only difficult part of this particular endeavor was imagining Margaret Hornor in the bedroom servicing the orange-shorted pasty-assed father of her child.

I tried not to think about that and instead ran through in my mind Margaret Hornor's decision to hire me.

So she starts off being married to a crooked white-collar investor. Well, wait. I tried to figure out the timeline in my head. If Molly was in her late teens or early twenties or so, which she appeared to be, and her sister was at Harvard, that made a certain kind of sense.

Because the social photos that I'd seen of Margaret Hornor and Boswell were around ten years old or so, by my guess. Maybe fifteen. That meant that Margaret had most likely either had an affair or had given birth to her children before she landed Boswell. Maybe she had been one of the Candyman's clients before cleaning herself up and landing a wealthy mover and shaker.

Maybe Boswell had adopted the girls, bequeathed a trust fund full of illegal money which was probably going to be taken away, and discovered that his wife was the one not on the up and up.

Maybe she was still in love with the Candyman, and continued to see him for sex and drugs after she'd married Boswell.

Now that really depressed me.

In any event, they were now cohorts as well as former lovers. If I believed Boswell, and I sort of did, they were trying to get at the trust fund money before the authorities confiscated it.

I noodled things around in my head for a while longer. Until I heard voices outside the door and then I got to my feet and stood behind the door.

When it opened and light spilled into the room, he wouldn't see me.

As I listened, it sounded like he and the black girl were arguing.

"You blew it," the black girl was saying. "Seriously, you're the worst drug dealer I've ever seen in my life. When are you gonna start doing it the way I say?"

There was no doubt in my mind that the black girl was much more dangerous than the pathetic excuse of a man known as the Candyman. So I drew the Colt and when the door opened and they both stepped inside, I put the muzzle of the gun directly against the back of her head.

"Nag, nag, nag," I said.

They both stopped.

The black girl was smart enough not to do anything. The Candyman practically jumped out of his flip-flops and looked like he was being attacked by a gang of fire ants.

I plucked the shiny little revolver out of the black girl's shorts and could see she had no other weapon, except maybe for her mouth. After pocketing the revolver, I used my free hand to open the door.

"Get your ass out of here and don't come back," I said. "This is gonna have a bad ending."

That's what I love about drug dealers. Absolutely no loyalty. She turned and scooted out of that place like she was late for a red carpet event. Like she'd been invited to the Oscars as a guest of Matt Damon.

I slammed the door shut and locked it.

The Candyman stood there, his knees shaking and I could see a line of sweat along his makeup-covered forehead.

"What's your real name, asshole?" I said. I pointed the gun at him.

He held up his hands. My guess was that he got manicures.

"Charles," he said. "Charles Laughlin."

"Sit on the bed, Chucky, and listen up," I said.

Then I put forth my best theory about his relationship with Margaret and their love children. Following that, the narrative went to Boswell and the pathetic scheme involving me to try to liberate Molly from the Chief.

"Have I got that about right, Chuckles?" I said.

"Yeah, so what? We didn't break any laws doing this," he whined at me. "Maggie's smart as a whip. You know one of our daughters is at Harvard, right?"

I rolled my eyes.

"I can't believe you're going to try to take credit for that," I said. "Look around you. You seriously think any of your daughter's intelligence comes from you? If they inherited your intelligence, they'd be studying textbooks on repairing dishwashers."

I was goading him a little bit, I'm not going to lie. But he had verified most of my theory. So in a sense I was done with him. But I did have one question left.

"When was the last time you saw Maggie?" I hated using that nickname. She was Margaret to me. The question wasn't really relevant to the case, it had more to do with my personal pride.

"I haven't seen that bitch in like a year," Charles spat. "She refuses to see me in person. We talk via text. Burner phones, usually. She doesn't want anything to do with me. She just wants that money."

That's how I'd figured it, too.

With an unhurried motion I acted like I was reaching for my cell phone but actually I swung the Colt in a short, but powerful arc.

The side of the heavy gun crashed into the Candyman's temple and he slid to the floor like a discarded banana peel.

I went and got the bag of drugs and taped it to his chest and tied his feet and legs with a lamp cord. Next, I took a picture of the Candyman in all of his drug-dealing glory and texted it to Barbieri along with the address.

And I added, "You're welcome."

Always the romantic, I was sure to include the little smiley face icon making a kissing face with a red heart.

26

Although there isn't much paperwork in my business, I'm quite good at it. So when I went back to my office, I quickly called up the contract I'd signed with Margaret Hornor and analyzed the end date.

She was essentially paying me by the week and we were three days from the end of it. A quick bit of math on the calculator and I had the amount to refund Margaret, based on my terminating the case.

Immediately.

A quick draft of an email notating the termination of our agreement and the subsequent refund was fired off to her email. I printed off a hard copy of both as well, just in case Miss Shady tried any financial shenanigans. I was just glad her checks didn't bounce, because it sure sounded like she had some issues.

That done, I called Hammerhead. Surprisingly, he picked up.

"Carver, what do you want?" he asked, sounding put upon.

"Don't sound so glad to hear from me," I said. "Maybe your Mom needs to remind you what a nice guy I am."

"Believe me, she reminds me every day."

In the background, I heard a little bit of music and the clinking of glasses.

"What bar are you at?" I asked.

"Shandy's," he replied. It was a hole in the wall just off Federal. "Hey, did you ever bump into those two guys who were rousting me at my house?"

"No, why would I?" It was the truth. I hadn't "bumped" into them. I'd killed one, if not both of them, and left their corpses in West Palm Beach. Where I'm from, that doesn't qualify as "bumping."

"It's just weird, no one's seen them," Hammerhead said.

"Now it's my turn for a question. What do you know about the Chief?"

Hammerhead nearly gasped. "Oh God, why

are you asking about him? Don't ask about him. Don't even talk about him. Dude's pure psychopath. He chainsawed some guy a few months back and used the pieces for shark bait."

"What else," I answered.

"You want more?"

"I want what you have."

"His main street dealer is a guy named Lonzo," Hammerhead said. "Works along the beach."

"How do I find him?" I asked.

"I thought you were after the Chief?"

"Answer the goddamn question."

"You can't miss him. He drives a G-Wagon all decked out in glitter. It's the gaudiest G-Wagon in Florida. It's too tacky for South Beach, even."

Someone yelled in the background.

"Look Carver, I gotta run, you need anything–"

Nope, I thought, as I hung up on him. *I've got everything I need.*

27

It wasn't going to be a needle in a haystack, exactly. There were a couple of things going for me. First off, a glittery G-Wagon would never qualify as a needle. Secondly, the stretch of the A1A that hugged the beach was long, I admit. However, parking was limited. There were some long stretches of parking spaces right on the A1A, but there were also a lot of public parking areas.

There was no doubt in my mind that Lonzo would want a space right on the beach. That's where the foot traffic was. That's where his G-Wagon would lure prospective buyers in. So, being able to immediately write off the public parking areas and stick to street parking made my task much more realistic.

Also helping me was that the Chief's "territory" wouldn't be huge. There was a lot of competition in his business, most likely marked by easily visible borders.

To the south, my starting point would be the Deerfield Beach Pier. It was a huge tourist attraction with a big beach, showers, and the pier itself, which was home to a lot of fishermen. It was also known as a good spot to buy drugs. My guess was that the Chief's territory didn't extend that far, but I wanted to be generous with my starting point.

My plan was to go all the way north, through Boca Raton, Highland Beach and Delray Beach until I reached Boynton Beach. Boynton was an even bigger drug town than Deerfield Beach. My guess was that the area between Deerfield and Boynton would be the Chief's main territory.

This time, I took the Scout for a slightly higher perspective and vantage point. Traffic wasn't bad, as it was late afternoon. Most of the foot traffic was coming off the beach as opposed to going in. However, this was when a lot of people liked to buy their drugs, getting ready for the evening ahead.

The A1A was busy, as always, by the Deerfield

Beach pier, but I slowly navigated my way through it, looking for Lonzo and his pimped out SUV.

No sign of him.

Deerfield gave way to Boca Raton, which didn't really have a beach strip, per se. There was a downtown, with a small public parking area. I cruised through that, didn't see anything, and moved on.

When I hit Delray Beach, the hunter in me kicked into high gear. This would be the heart of his territory and the most likely spot for me to find Lonzo. Suddenly, I saw the telltale shape of a G-Wagon and leaned forward, until I pulled alongside it and saw it was painted a jet black, with an older white couple occupying the front seats, arguing with each other.

The rest of Delray showed no signs of my quarry and I made it all the way to Boynton Beach, where traffic picked up once again. There were a lot more users here, and many of them in much rougher shape than their counterparts in Delray. Which was funny because Delray had more rehab centers than anywhere else. Maybe they left rehab in Delray and landed in Boynton to score.

After a thorough canvas of the beach vehicles, and another G-Wagon, this one silver, I turned around and started the whole process over again. I figured it might take me two or three trips before it got too dark and then I would have to start again the next day.

It was on the third round-trip that a G-Wagon passed me. It was behind a Range Rover and I almost missed it, but there was no doubt.

It was Lonzo in all of his glittery glory.

A quick turn took me off the A1A where I did a quick U-turn, barreled back onto the road, and caught up to him as he was parking. At this time of day, there were quite a few parking spaces available.

I pulled past him and parked the Scout, then got out and walked back to him.

A quick glance told me there were no police nearby, and traffic was slow. The Range Rover had gone on ahead.

Traffic had subsided.

Lonzo was already out of the G-Wagon, and along with another man, was standing on the side-walk, both looking at their phones.

That's one of the things I loved about cell phones. Oh, people complain about them all the time. How everyone is driving or texting. Or no one talks anymore. The art of conversation is dead, thanks to the phones.

Me, I loved them.

People everywhere just *weren't paying attention.*

They were staring at their phones.

It made classic assault & battery so simple.

The bodyguard had his back to me and I threw a right hook from my waist, everything behind it and caught him just under the ear, where the jaw connects to the back of the skull. I swung through the punch and the man dropped to the sidewalk, his head bouncing off the cement. He was probably out from the punch, but the head slam into the concrete sidewalk made sure of it.

I let the punch carry me through and directly into Lonzo.

"What the f..." he started to say.

My left hand came up under my right and I caught Lonzo by the wrist. I brought my right arm back, elbow pointed out and simultaneously pulled him toward me. He leaned his head back and my elbow caught him on the temple. It was more of a glancing blow, though, and he staggered back, reaching for a gun.

Although kicks to the groin are overdone in Hollywood movies, it was the right choice at the moment. My right arm had swung through, my left arm was still pulling Lonzo toward me and that meant my balance was perfect to launch a good, hard kick into the drug dealer's balls.

He immediately shrunk into himself, like a balloon being popped. I finished pulling him into me, reached around, got the gun he was going for and then "helped" him to the G-Wagon. I pulled open the passenger side door and pushed him in, like he was a buddy who'd gotten drunk at the beach and now needed help getting into the car.

However, I had no intention of keeping him with me. I head-butted him a really nasty blow on the bridge of his nose and his eyes rolled back into his head and his phone clattered to the ground.

He didn't weigh much so I hoisted him over my shoulder and carried him over to a bench meant for beachgoers who wanted to sit and adjust their gear before or after their day in the sun. His body-guard soon joined him and it looked like they were slumped back, chilling. I'd retrieved sunglasses from the G-Wagon and fitted them onto Lonzo. A cop might notice their lack of movement, but that would take awhile.

The G-Wagon's keys were now in my possession, along with Lonzo's and his bodyguard's cell phones.

I fired up the big vehicle and pointed it toward my favorite beachfront compound.

It was time to find the Chief.

And get some answers.

28

The G-Wagon featured a neat little brush guard on the front that I planned to use to help me bash through the gates of the Chief's compound. I also shifted the big vehicle into four-wheel drive low for additional torque. Not really a good idea to do that on pavement, but I was just borrowing the SUV. Long-term damage wasn't really my concern.

Of course, it also occurred to me that the G-Wagon would most likely be equipped with a remote control or a built-in sensor that could cause the gate to open automatically. There were even some additional buttons near the dome lights that I knew could be pre-programmed.

Guessing that would be the case, I approached

the gates slowly and waited a beat.

The gate did not open.

I glanced up at the buttons. There were three in a row near the interior light above the rearview mirror. Upon closer inspection, the one in the middle looked like it was slightly more worn than the other two.

I pressed it.

The gate opened.

A circular driveway welcomed me and my glittery ride into the realm of the Chief. There was a Rolls-Royce already parked near what appeared to be the main entrance to the home. The middle of the circular drive was home to fruit trees. Oranges and maybe a star fruit. Lights illuminated the winding drive.

The security guard I'd seen earlier emerged from the shadows of an arched structured covered in bougainvillea. He had the requisite black T-shirt, black shorts, and a gun belt.

He glanced out, saw the G-Wagon, and then stepped back and was lost in the shadows.

I slid across the front seat and exited the vehicle from the passenger side, blocking any clear views of me as I walked along the circular path toward the spot where the security guard was.

Just before I got to the entrance, I shuffled my feet so he could hear me. He stepped out again and I punched him in the throat, just above the top of his bulletproof vest, just below his double chin. He gasped and his hands went to his throat. I grabbed him by the vest, did a leg sweep, and dropped him to the ground.

He started writhing, so I took out his ridiculously long flashlight and clobbered him over the head with it.

He stopped moving.

From his gun belt I took a Taser, a Glock pistol, and his walkie talkie. I checked that the Glock was loaded, and held it in front of me, along with the walkie talkie. The Taser I'd slipped into my pocket.

The first surprise was that the main doors into the house were unguarded. They were oversized wood doors, elaborately carved with a pattern that seemed to me to indicate a South Pacific style.

Samoan, no doubt.

A few theories went through my head regarding why the main door was left alone. They'd seen me coming. Video cameras saw me take down the perimeter guard.

Those guesses were all wrong.

Because once I was inside, I heard voices. A

shout or two. I passed silently through a foyer, a great room with a towering fireplace and twenty-foot high ceilings, then into the kitchen. It, too, was massive. Big enough for a staff of ten. But the real draw was a stairwell at the back of the room.

Another black T-shirted big guy stood with his back to the kitchen, facing the commotion down-stairs. I pulled the Taser from my pocket, stepped up, and blasted him in the neck with fifty thou-sand volts. I chose the neck to make sure he didn't scream. He started to fall forward so I let go of the Taser, caught him and pulled him back into the kitchen and dropped him to the floor.

Slowly, I descended the stairs, stepping into a well-lit room with tile floors and industrial sinks on one side of the room, a pegboard with various tools on the other.

In the middle stood the Chief. He had a big knife in his hand and there were two men on the floor, bound and covered in blood.

They looked dead.

Flanking the Chief was one of his men. He had a shotgun in his hand, and had caught some of the blood splatter.

Off to the side was another person, also bound.
Molly.

29

The room exploded as soon as the Chief saw me. He swung his big head around and started walking toward me.

"You," he said, his voice flat and without surprise.

His assistant torturer started to lift the shotgun so I shot him first with the Glock. A double-tap, center mass. It knocked him backward and the shotgun fired into the air, knocking off chunks of plaster.

The Chief never slowed. He showed no signs of fear or hesitation. He was five feet away when I shot out his left kneecap. He tottered to his right to compensate, and I destroyed his other knee with a second shot.

He fell forward, still holding onto the knife. I aimed at the arm holding the knife and shot out his elbow. The knife clattered to the ground. I quickly stepped around him and picked it up.

"What the hell is this?" I asked. It was like a machete, but with a weird curl of metal at the end.

"His fire knife," Molly said from the side of the room. "He loves that thing. A family heirloom or something stupid."

"No escape," the Chief said. "You're not going to–"

I used the butt of the knife and drove it into his temple so hard it sounded like a meat cleaver hitting bone, which I guess it sort of was.

He went face-first into the tile and I walked over to Molly.

I used the curled tip of the knife to cut her restraints and she got to her feet.

"Who the hell are you, anyway?" she asked.

From my pocket I took out the G-Wagon's keys. "How about you take off? Stay away from Mom and the Candyman. They're after your inheritance."

"I know," she said, rubbing her wrists. "It's in a safe place. Divided up and redistributed. Even the cops can't get at it if they try."

She glanced over at the Chief. "He was after it, too, once he found out. Someone must have given him the heads-up because all of a sudden he started looking at me weird. I was going to be the next on the torture block, I think."

"Sounds about right," I said. I took out my phone and clicked on the picture of my sister. "Do you know her? Her name is Jenny. Jenny Carver. Have you ever seen her?"

She looked and shook her head. "No. Sorry. I would tell you if I had." She lifted her chin toward the Chief. "He would, though. He makes it a point of knowing every single female who comes to the beach looking for drugs."

"Okay," I said. "You need to leave. Now."

Molly ran from the room and I walked over to the Chief. He was groggy, but coming to. Over by the sink I saw a bottle of Dom Perignon. I popped the cork, walked over and poured it onto his face. He sputtered and then his eyes opened.

I showed him the picture of my sister.

"Where is she?"

He gave a smile or a grimace, I wasn't sure which.

"Go to hell," he said.

I lined up the fire knife along his right wrist.

"Try again," I said.

"I don't recognize her without my dick in her mouth," he said.

I raised the big knife in my hand and chopped down with it. Hard.

Thunk.

The knife easily sliced through the Chief's wrist and his hand was now severed. Blood gushed from the stump of his arm.

"Try again."

He raised the stump, looked for his hand and started to yell.

I looked over at his other hand. Raised the knife.

Thunk.

Matching stumps now.

"Hey look, you're a hands-free device," I pointed out.

The yelling continued, and this time, I understood what he said.

It took him ten minutes to bleed out. I wiped my prints from the knife and placed it in the hand of the Chief's sidekick, who I'd shot in the chest.

The two dead men in the center of the room who the Chief had been torturing were probably rival drug dealers.

I pulled their bodies next to the Chief's. I wiped off the Glock and put it in the Chief's hand, then did the same with the Taser and left it in the third man's hand.

Nothing else had been touched, so I left the room, walked back out the way I had come in and left through the door by the side of the entrance gate.

The Scout was a ten-minute walk and as I put one foot in front of the other, the Chief's final words had echoed in my head.

"She's bad. Bad," he'd screamed.

There were a lot of ways to take that. To my right, I could hear the ocean's waves pounding into the sand. The night stars were out and the warm breeze from the water began to cleanse me of the scene in the basement.

Still, the Chief's last words swirled in my brain, ignorant to the breeze.

"They call her–" he'd gasped, blood streaming from his arms.

"Call her what?" I'd asked.

And with the last word he would ever utter, the Chief died with my sister's new name on his lips.

"Sugar."

WADE CARVER THRILLER # 2!

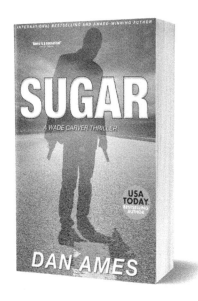

CLICK HERE TO BUY

ABOUT THE AUTHOR

Dan Ames is a USA TODAY Bestselling Author and winner of the Independent Book Award for Crime Fiction.

www.authordanames.com

dan@authordanames.com

A USA TODAY BESTSELLING BOOK

The JACK REACHER Cases CLICK HERE

ALSO BY DAN AMES

The JACK REACHER Cases #1 (A Hard Man To Forget)

The JACK REACHER Cases #2 (The Right Man For Revenge)

The JACK REACHER Cases #3 (A Man Made For Killing)

DEAD WOOD (John Rockne Mystery #1)

HARD ROCK (John Rockne Mystery #2)

COLD JADE (John Rockne Mystery #3)

LONG SHOT (John Rockne Mystery #4)

EASY PREY (John Rockne Mystery #5)

BODY BLOW (John Rockne Mystery #6)

THE KILLING LEAGUE (Wallace Mack Thriller #1)

THE MURDER STORE (Wallace Mack Thriller #2)

FINDERS KILLERS (Wallace Mack Thriller #3)

DEATH BY SARCASM (Mary Cooper Mystery #1)

MURDER WITH SARCASTIC INTENT (Mary Cooper Mystery #2)

GROSS SARCASTIC HOMICIDE (Mary Cooper Mystery #3)

KILLER GROOVE (Rockne & Cooper Mystery #1)

BEER MONEY (Burr Ashland Mystery #1)

THE CIRCUIT RIDER (Circuit Rider #1)

KILLER'S DRAW (Circuit Rider #2)

TO FIND A MOUNTAIN (A WWII Thriller)

STANDALONE THRILLERS:

THE RECRUITER

KILLING THE RAT

HEAD SHOT

THE BUTCHER

BOX SETS:

AMES TO KILL

GROSSE POINTE PULP

GROSSE POINTE PULP 2

TOTAL SARCASM

WALLACE MACK THRILLER COLLECTION

SHORT STORIES:

THE GARBAGE COLLECTOR

BULLET RIVER

SCHOOL GIRL

HANGING CURVE

SCALE OF JUSTICE

FREE BOOKS AND MORE

Would you like a FREE copy of my story BULLET RIVER?

Then sign up for the DAN AMES BOOK CLUB:

For special offers and new releases, sign up here

Made in United States
Orlando, FL
03 March 2024